Rory covered her eyes with both hands, fighting back tears.

"There's so much, Felix. There's just so much. I can't... I don't..." But her words and thoughts both trailed off before she could complete any of them.

"Hey, hey, hey," she heard him say. "It's okay, Rory."

He scooted closer to her, wrapped an arm around her shoulders and pulled her close. She melted into him, fighting back more tears. There really was just so much. So many memories. So many feelings.

Too many memories. Too many feelings. Not the least of which was how this was going to change whatever was happening between her and Felix. Things had just started feeling pretty good between them.

Now she was someone else. Someone with a past. Someone with a history. Someone he might not like as much as he liked her before.

Because she was pretty sure he'd liked her before. Maybe even as much as she liked him...

Dear Reader,

I love to cook. Especially international dishes. So when Cuban American chef Felix Suarez ambled into my brain, I was delighted. So many Cuban dishes to look up on the internet! So many Cuban dishes to try myself! I could eat *huevos habaneros* every morning for the rest of my life. Especially if Felix were in my kitchen making it. Ahem.

Rory Vincent, on the other hand, is... Well, there's the problem. Rory doesn't really know *what* she is. Or who she is. She can't remember anything prior to an accident nine months ago. But there's something about Felix that rattles a few memories out of her brain. Soon, he's rattling a whole lot more...

I hope you have as much fun reading about Felix and Rory as I had writing them. And seriously, try the *huevos* habaneros.

Happy eating! I mean reading!

Elizabeth

Her Good-Luck Charm

ELIZABETH BEVARLY

ISBN-13: 978-1-335-72424-3

Her Good-Luck Charm

For questions and comments about the quality of this book, please contact us at CustomerService@Harlequin.com.

Harlequin Enterprises ULC
22 Adelaide St. West, 41st Floor
Toronto, Ontario M5H 4E3, Canada
www.Harlequin.com

Printed in U.S.A.

Elizabeth Bevarly is the award-winning *New York Times* bestselling author of more than seventy books, novellas and screenplays. Although she has called places like San Juan, Puerto Rico, and Haddonfield, New Jersey, home, she's now happily settled back in her native Kentucky with her husband and son. When she's not writing, she's binge-watching documentaries on Netflix, spending too much time on Reddit or making soup out of whatever she finds in the freezer. Visit her at elizabethbevarly.com for news about current and upcoming projects; book, music and film recommendations; recipes; and lots of other fun stuff.

Books by Elizabeth Bevarly

Harlequin Special Edition

Lucky Stars

Be Careful What You Wish For

Harlequin Desire

Taming the Prince
Taming the Beastly M.D.
Married to His Business
The Billionaire Gets His Way
My Fair Billionaire
Caught in the Billionaire's Embrace

Accidental Heirs

Only on His Terms
A CEO in Her Stocking
The Pregnancy Affair
A Beauty for the Billionaire
Baby in the Making

Visit the Author Profile page
at Harlequin.com for more titles.

For Charles Griemsman.

Thanks for *always* making me a better writer.

I owe you lunch at a Cuban restaurant someday.

Prologue

Fifteen-year-old Felix Suarez loved the smell of *sofrito* in the morning. Or the afternoon. Or the evening. He wasn't particular. He just loved his grandmother's sofrito that much. And because his *tita* owned and operated the most popular Cuban restaurant in southern Indiana—for all he knew, it was the only Cuban restaurant in southern Indiana—and because her sofrito was the basis of so many of her recipes, the little apartment the two of them shared above La Mariposa smelled like sofrito pretty much all the time. Food of the gods, that was what it was. The peppers, the onion, the garlic, the cilantro…

"Holy crow, what smells so good?"

The question came from one of Felix's best friends, Max Travers, who was just waking up from where he'd been sleeping on the living room floor nearby.

"Food of the gods," Felix told him. Because that bore repeating, even if it had only been in his head the first time.

"It's Señora Suarez's sofrito," his other best friend, Chance Foley, clarified from his own spot on the floor on Max's other side.

"Ya know," Max said, "I didn't think anything could smell better than my mom's *doro wat*, but your grandmother could give her a run for her money."

"Tita and your mom should have a cook-off," Felix said. "Cuba versus Ethiopia. We could sell tickets and make a fortune, and I could finally get out of this boring town."

"I'd buy the hell out of an event like that," Chance said. "Meanwhile, my mom promised to make meatloaf tonight." Dryly, he added, "Yay."

"Hey, your mom's meatloaf is da bomb," Max assured his friend.

The three boys had spent the night together at Felix's place following the Galaxy Ball at Mrs. Barclay's mansion—the final, crowning event of the Welcome Back, Bob comet festival that happened in their hometown of Endicott, Indiana, for the first few weeks of September every fifteen years. Comet Bob—who actually had a much longer name, but it was one hardly anyone could pronounce—visited Earth every fifteen years, and when it did, it always made its closest pass directly above Endicott, Indiana. No one knew why. Truth be told, at this point, no one cared why. Over the past couple centuries, though, the town had come to claim the comet as its own, and it went all out to welcome Bob back every decade and a half, with events and parties and revelry that went on for weeks.

"Tita uses sofrito in a ton of her recipes," Felix said. He hesitated a moment before adding, "Except sometimes I think maybe she should use Spanish onions instead of yellow. And maybe go just a *little* heavier on the Cubanelle peppers and a *little* lighter on the green peppers. But that's just me."

Not that Felix would ever even suggest to Tita that she change a single thing about her cooking. She'd taught him everything she knew—and she knew a lot. Someday, Felix was going to open his own restaurant—and he'd do it someplace way more exciting than Endicott, that was for sure—and then he could experiment all he wanted with what he'd learned from her. Here and now, though, the recipes of La Mariposa were sacred.

He just wished the here and now was anywhere but Endicott and anytime but the present. This town was the most monotonous place on the planet. He didn't care if there was a major festival going on at the moment. This time next week, all the festivities would be over, and all the visitors would be trickling away. Endicott would go back to being its usual tedious self, where the most exciting things to happen were discovering a forgotten dollar in your pants pocket or scoring an extra couple of Tater Tots on the school cafeteria lunch line.

It was why Felix had made the wish he had on the comet this week. There were a lot of legends that had risen up about Bob over the centuries. That the comet created cosmic disturbances that made people say and do things they normally wouldn't, or fall in love with people they normally wouldn't give the time of day to, or make amends over generations-old feuds. But Felix's favorite was the one about the wishes. He'd heard all his life—and so had every other kid born the year Bob came around last time—that he granted wishes to those who were born in a year of the comet. As in, if someone was born in a year Bob passed over Endicott, and if that someone made a wish the next time the comet came around, when they were fifteen, then on Bob's third pass, when the person was thirty, he'd make that wish come true.

Felix, Max and Chance were all comet kids, born the last time Bob came around. And they'd all made wishes three nights ago, when Bob was reported to be at his closest point overhead. Chance had wished for a million dollars. Max had wished his crush, Marcy Hanlon, would see him as something other than the kid who took care of their lawn. Blah blah blah. Felix's wish was one that had real promise, and one that could help out all three of them. Because Felix had wished that, just once, something *interesting* would happen in Endicott. This town was long overdue for some decent action.

It was just too bad he'd have to wait fifteen years for it to happen. Especially since he had every plan to beat it out of town as soon as he could and go someplace where interesting stuff happened all the time. Indianapolis, maybe. Or Cincinnati. Hell, even Louisville, across the river, would be good. Someplace where people didn't call it a day as soon as the sun went down.

Yeah, something interesting. Was that too much to ask? Even though Bob was now beating his retreat from Earth and Endicott, Felix sent one more reminder heavenward. He closed his eyes and thought hard. *Something* interesting, *Bob. That's all I ask. Doesn't matter* how *it's interesting. Only that it* is. *It can be a person, a thing, an event, whatever you want. Just make it interesting. Please. For the love of all things cosmic, just please make it* interesting.

Chapter One

Fifteen Years Later...

Felix Suarez was about to unlock the front door of his restaurant when he noticed the guy—Tracksuit Guy—hanging out in an alley across the street. Again. Despite the fact that Septembers in southern Indiana could still be pretty warm, the guy was always in a tracksuit. Usually black with gold stripes, but sometimes he got flashy and showed up in maroon with red. For more than a week, the guy had been a regular fixture on Water Street, the main drag of the historic district in Endicott, Indiana, populated by dozens of local businesses.

At first, Felix had figured the guy was in town for the Welcome Back, Bob comet festival, which hadn't even officially kicked off yet, but for which a lot of people arrived in town as soon as the comet was spotted on the horizon. He'd remembered how, the last time Bob came around, fifteen years ago, when Felix was fifteen himself, the die-hard comet fans had started arriving before the festivities even started, along with the best telescopes money could buy at Radio Shack. But this year, with this guy, as the days had gone on…

Ay, dios mío. As the days went on, Felix had decided there was something about this guy that didn't quite mesh with the other visitors to town. He didn't seem festive. He didn't look happy. He didn't appear to be interested in going anywhere in Endicott other than that alley across the street. And he seemed way too intense, too focused, to be up to any good.

Felix had actually started entertaining the idea that the guy was watching his restaurant and might be casing the place. It wasn't as if he was making millions with La Mariposa, but he was doing very well. He'd brought the restaurant along a lot since his grandmother's death two years ago, and it was a rare night when it wasn't packed. If somebody wanted to rob a local business, La Mariposa was as likely a target as any.

The owner of a small business, even in a town as quiet as this one, couldn't be too careful.

Eventually, however, Felix had realized the guy wasn't watching his restaurant. He was watching the business next door—Wallflowers, a florist. A florist that had just opened a little over a month ago and was barely making ends meet, as far as Felix could tell. So why was a would-be thief scoping it out? Unless maybe he wasn't a would-be thief scoping out a possible target for theft, but maybe *was* a would-be stalker scoping out Wallflowers's owner. Because one thing Wallflowers did have going for it was its proprietress, Rory Vincent. Five feet, ten inches of smoking-hot, icy-cool deliciousness, from the ends of her close-cropped, inky black hair to the tips of her cotton candy–pink toenails.

A stalker could definitely do worse, because Rory Vincent was, hands down, the most interesting human being Felix had ever met. Even though she'd only been living in Endicott for a couple of months, she'd been the talk of the town from the minute she arrived. Rhodes Scholar, sharpshooter, onetime Olympic hopeful, former aerialist for Cirque du Soleil, climbed Mount Kilimanjaro… Every time anyone had a conversation with her, they learned something more fascinating about her than whatever tidbit they'd heard before. And, naturally, the information spread like wildfire, since gossiping was pretty much the town's favorite pastime. Felix didn't think anyone in Endicott had achieved even one of the things Rory had. Yet here was a single individual who had done them all. He probably should be surprised if she *didn't* have a stalker.

He hadn't seen Tracksuit Guy for a couple of days, though, so he'd started to think he must be wrong about the skulking around and that the guy had finally moved on to other interests. Or maybe he'd just been waiting for more comet festivities to begin. But now Tracksuit Guy was back in the alley across the street. And he was watching Rory's place again. Like Felix, she lived in an apartment above her shop, so her workplace was her living space, too. And something about the guy watching Rory's life in its completeness that way sent a ripple of unease down his spine.

Instead of unlocking his front door—opening was still hours away anyway—he headed back to the kitchen, where his staff was busily prepping for Saturday brunch. His chef de cuisine, Tinima, was looking over the delivery from a local organic farm, her thick black-and-silver braid wound snugly around her head.

"'Morning, Chef," she said when she saw him.

"Hey, Tinima. How does the broccoli rabe look for the *harina*?"

"Perfect," she told him. Then she glanced up, her dark eyes shining mischievously. "Why? Thinking of taking some next door to Rory after the brunch rush?"

He bit back an irritated sound. That question in some form had come pretty regularly from Tinima since Rory Vincent opened her business next door.

"No," he told her. "I just remember last week, we had to toss a good quarter of it out. I don't want to have to substitute asparagus again. That was *no bueno*."

"Oh, right, sure," Tinima said, smiling like the all-knowing goddess that she was. "I forgot."

Chefs de cuisine. *Dios mío.*

Felix ventured farther into the kitchen to find his pastry chef, Arjun, putting the finishing touches on the *pastelitos de guayaba* before they went into the oven. The guava pastries had been some of their most popular brunch selections since Arjun became the one baking them.

"Hey there, Chef," Arjun said when he noted Felix's approach, even though his attention never shifted from the pastries he was so carefully arranging in a sheet pan.

"'Morning, Arjun," Felix replied. He paused

briefly to admire the pastry chef's creations. "Lookin' good, my dude."

Arjun smiled. "Thanks." He dropped the last of the confections into the pan, then reached for a bowl of what looked like some kind of cream filling. "I was thinking of adding some queso fresco and a little turbinado to the pastelitos. See what you think."

Felix grabbed a spoon and tipped it with the creamy mixture, then tasted it. Normally, he didn't want to veer from the recipes they used on their most popular items. But this could work.

"It's good," he told Arjun. "Tell you what we'll do. For every order of regular pastelitos that leaves the kitchen today, we'll send out, gratis, a sample of one with the new filling. Have the servers tell their customers we're curious about which one they like best and see which one performs better. If it does well, we'll make it a permanent fixture on the menu. Call it Pastelitos Arjunito or something."

Arjun nodded his approval with the moniker as he returned the bowl to the counter. "You should take some of the new pastelitos over to Rory after the rush," he told Felix. "She's a pastry fiend."

Felix shook his head. Arjun, too? "Maybe you could take her some," he said.

Arjun grinned at him in much the same way

Tinima had. Felix did his best not to smack him upside his head.

Pastry chefs. *Dios mío.*

"Have you seen Chloe this morning?" he asked.

"Over here!" he heard his head hostess call out in response.

He turned around to find her pulling a tray of vases out of the Hobart, their varicolored glass beaded with moisture from the dishwasher steam. Chloe was beaded, too, doubtless because the temperature in the kitchen was already nearing triple digits. She wasn't much bigger than the tray she was wrestling with, but she hoisted it expertly onto one shoulder and began heading for the front of the house.

"What do you need, Chef?" she asked as she went.

Felix intercepted her and easily took the tray from her, ignoring her protest that she could manage it just fine. Yes, she could. But c'mon.

"Have you picked up today's stems from Wallflowers yet?" he asked as they entered the dining room.

"It's next on my list."

"Don't worry about it. I'll take care of it this morning."

Chloe smiled the same way Tinima and Arjun had moments ago, her gray eyes practically sparkling. Like everyone else who worked at La Mariposa, she thought he had a thing for Rory Vincent. What the hell was everyone's problem?

"It's not like what you're thinking," he told her.

She feigned confusion. "What am I thinking?"

"That I have a thing for Rory."

"Why would I think that?" she asked in her best *pshaw* voice. "The super busy executive-chef-slash-owner of the region's hottest restaurant—the one who has three James Beard Awards—*always* picks up the flowers for the day's tables, since everyone knows table flowers are the key to any restaurant's success, and it has nothing to do with the quality of the food or service."

Felix stifled a growl. "I just need to talk to Rory about something, that's all."

"Of course you do, Chef."

Hostesses. *Dios mío.*

He threw an exaggerated glare at Chloe, then spun silently on the rubber heel of his chef clogs. Whatever. Deluders gonna delude.

He headed back to the kitchen, asking Tinima to keep an eye on things until he got back, ignoring both the smugness in her smile and her smart-ass tone when she told him, "If you can't be good, be careful." Then he headed out the back door, into the alley that connected the four storefronts on this side of this block of Water Street.

He wasn't surprised to see the back entrance of Wallflowers open, too. Rory's workday started long before his did—and generally ended earlier, too. In an hour or so, when she opened, there would be a handful of additional people working with her, but at the moment, only her senior arranger, Ezra, was at work in the back room. When Felix saw him, he rapped his knuckles on the doorframe. Ezra looked up and smiled. He was the antithesis of Rory, obsidian and bantam to her ivory and elevation—seriously, she stood nearly eye to eye with Felix, who topped six feet himself. Ezra's personality was the opposite of Rory's, too, warm and relaxed to her cool and formal.

But then, Felix had always liked the cool, formal ones. They were more of a challenge. And he'd never met a challenge he couldn't overcome. Eventually.

"What's up, Felix?" Ezra asked as he beckoned him in.

Like the kitchen of Mariposa, the back room of Wallflowers smelled amazing. Sweetness from the flowers mingled with savory from the greenery, some of the aromas mild, some pungent, some light, some dark. Unlike like his overwhelmingly silver-and-white kitchen, however, color was everywhere here, from the reds and pinks of the roses to the purples and yellows of the tulips. Not for the first time, he was struck by how he and Rory both made their livings from things that grew out of the ground, but in entirely different ways.

"Is Rory around?" he asked.

Ezra sobered at the question, clearly noting his concern. "Yeah, she's out front. Everything okay?"

"Tracksuit Guy is back," Felix told him.

He knew Ezra would know who he was talking about, since Tracksuit Guy had become the topic of a number of conversations among the business owners and their employees on this part of Water Street. Veronica, who owned a vintage shop at the end of the block, had even called the cops on him at one point, and they'd had a chat with the guy during one of his appearances. But he'd assured them he was only in town for the comet festival and just happened to really like the businesses on that block. Since hanging out wasn't a crime, the cops hadn't been able to do anything about him. Interesting, though, how none of the owners of the businesses he'd claimed to love had ever seen him inside their respective businesses. Really interesting, as far as Felix was concerned.

Ezra went back to arranging his flowers. "Well, she's not going to be happy about it. But she's not going to be surprised, either."

It was an interesting response. So was Ezra's nonchalance. He was acting as if Rory knew the guy or something.

Felix gestured toward the door on the other side of the room, the one that led to the store itself. "Do you mind…?" he asked.

"Go ahead," Ezra told him. "It's looking to be a slow morning for a Saturday. I think she's just restocking right now."

"Thanks," Felix replied as he headed in that direction.

The front of the store was dimly lit in advance of opening, but Felix found Rory easily enough near the counter, down on all fours, reaching into a cabinet for something she couldn't quite get a grip on. She was wearing the same thing she wore every day—jeans and a T-shirt, this one the dark chocolate brown of a sunflower's center. The same color as her eyes, he couldn't help thinking. Rory Vincent did have some super-dark—super-sexy—eyes, he had to say. Paired with her short black hair, not to mention the *keep your distance* aura she always exuded, the features imbued her with a cryptic sort of allure it was impossible for him to ignore.

"So, Rory," he called out, purposefully raising his voice louder than he needed to, just to get a start out of her.

It worked great, because she twitched enough to bump her head softly on the cabinet above her. Felix smiled. Doing stuff like that was the only way he could ever get a reaction out of her. When it came to her dealings with him, she was even more aloof than she was with other people.

"Dammit, Felix," she muttered as she straightened onto her knees. *Dios mío*, even at half-mast, she was tall. She rubbed the back of her head, despite the fact that she'd barely tapped it. "What do you want?"

Well, now there was a loaded question. Felix wanted a lot of things. World peace. A healthy work-life balance. Pay equity. To see Rory dressed like a French maid. The list could go on forever.

What he told her, however, was, "Tracksuit Guy is back."

Her gaze went instantly to her front door, and her expression changed from irritation to… Concern? Apprehension? Fear? Nine times out of ten, it was impossible to tell exactly what Rory was thinking.

She expelled a sound of… Concern? Apprehension? Fear? Then stood and went to her front door. Just as Felix had done moments before, she gazed out the window at the Water Street intruder. Then she turned around and looked at him.

"'Kay. Thanks. Bye," she said.

Okay, *eight* times out of ten it was impossible to tell exactly what Rory was thinking. Because her thoughts at the moment were pretty clear. She wanted him to scram. Which was too damned bad, because Felix wasn't quite ready to.

"Hey, you should come next door when you get a chance this morning," he told her. "Arjun is doing something special with the pastelitos, and you really need to try La Mariposa's pastelitos."

She really needed to try anything at La Mariposa, he thought. Including its chef. Especially its chef. But she'd actively avoided the place—and him—even though both were right next door.

She moved back to where he'd found her and kneeled in front of the cabinet again. "Thanks, but today's looking to be pretty busy."

"That's not what Ezra said."

She threw him a look. Okay, *seven* times out of ten it was impossible to tell what Rory was thinking.

"Fine," he said, "I'll bring some over to you after the brunch rush."

"Thanks," she replied grudgingly. She wasn't stupid, after all. Only an idiot would turn down free pastelitos. She reached back into the cabinet, grappling for something that was clearly beyond her grasp. Felix continued to lean in the doorway, letting her struggle, until she looked up at him with much aggravation.

"What?" she demanded.

"Need some help?"

He could see that she wanted to tell him no. But Ezra was the only other person in the shop at the moment, and his reach was even more limited than hers.

Finally, more grudgingly than before, she said, "If you don't mind."

Felix smiled. "Of course not!" As he approached her, he added, "Like I told you that first day you moved in next door, anything you need, Rory, you just let me know."

At the time, he'd been thinking more in terms of physical needs than professional ones, but hey, he'd take what he could get.

She moved out of his way—actually, she took three giant steps backward—and Felix assumed the position she'd had before. "What is it you're trying to get to?"

"There are three little clay pots at the very back. I need all three of them." As an afterthought, and with more grudgery, she added, "Please."

He easily plucked them out one by one and set them on the cabinet. Still down on his knees, he asked, "Need anything else?" Like, for instance… oh, he didn't know…a flirtatious wink? A coy innuendo? A sensuous touch? Hours and hours of exhaustive lovemaking? 'Cause Felix was up for pretty much anything, brunch rush be damned.

"I'm good," she told him.

She certainly was. In fact, Rory Vincent was the best thing to happen to Endicott in Felix's entire lifetime. Not for the first time in recent weeks, he remembered the wish he'd made on a comet when he was fifteen years old. He'd begged Comet Bob to make something *interesting* happen this year in a town where nothing interesting ever happened. And he couldn't help thinking now that the comet was definitely making good on that wish. First Rory's arrival in town, then her stalker. And now, even more interesting, her reaction to her stalker. Something about her reaction just now made it seem like she really did know him. Or, at least, she didn't seem to be surprised by his appearance. And her lack of alarm at his presence was the most interesting thing of all. Just what the hell was going on between Rory and Tracksuit Guy?

It was going to be interesting trying to figure that out.

Rory Vincent looked at Felix Suarez down on his knees in front of her—even if he was a good five feet away from her—and tried really, really,

really hard not to think about what she was thinking about at the moment. But the more she tried to banish the graphic images tumbling through her brain, the more erotic they became. And that way lay madness. And sweatiness. And extremely bothersome dreams. Dreams that had been coming and going for weeks—ever since she moved in next door to him and his restaurant. And every night on the days she'd had contact with him. Tonight, she was sure, would be no different.

She wondered why he was still there. She'd just told him she was good, hadn't she? So why was he just kneeling there, looking at her as if she wasn't? Why was he looking at her as if she were way better than good? As if she were, in fact, some confection even more delectable than La Mariposa's pastelitos, a confection that he couldn't wait to consume? And not in one big bite, as one would normally do with a delectable confection, but in lots of slow, enticing, exhaustive…oh, baby, so exhaustive…nibbles?

"So…" she began, stringing the single syllable out over several time zones. "Guess you need to be getting back to the restaurant, right? Almost time for brunch."

He stood, but he didn't make any move toward the door. Which was what she really needed him to do. There was only so much a woman could take when she was in the presence of a bronze god, and Rory was nearing the end of her rope. Because, as smooth and smug as Felix Suarez was, it was all encased in goldenness that looked as if it had been wrought by the hands of the gods. Truly, everything about him was gilded, from his dark blond hair, to his amber eyes, to his sun-burnished skin. She tried to tell herself that that was all Felix Suarez was, too—gilt. Something that only pretended to be fine and rare and dear. But there was something about him that was just so…

She pushed the thought away before she allowed it to form. Jeez, even his chef's jacket was gold, topping baggy pants spattered with tiny green and blue butterflies—for which his restaurant was named. *Felix* was stitched high on his chest on the jacket's left side, but as far as Rory was concerned, it might as well have identified him as "Adonis." Seriously, he had to get out of her shop *now*. Before she had an impromptu orgasm just looking at him.

It was amazing that she could be so physically attracted to someone she barely knew. And the little she did know didn't exactly make her want to learn more. He was just too…smooth. Too confident. Too slick. The kind of guy who knew the effect he had on women and capitalized on it. Then took advantage of it. Then trampled all over its intended targets. Rory didn't even want to think about how many notches there were on his bed-post. She wasn't about to become another one. Even if her body might have a different opinion about that.

"Brunch is still hours away," he told her. Not moving.

"Well, I open in less than an hour," she said.

She figured it was a pretty obvious indication that he should leave, but he still didn't move. He only smiled. She tried not to spontaneously com-bust.

"Okay," he said. Still not moving. "I'll come by after brunch with the new pastelitos. I'd really love to know what you think about them."

Yeah, well, she'd really love for him to get out of her store.

"Great," she said. She started to add that she looked forward to it—which she did—but didn't want to give him the wrong impression. Like maybe she was looking forward to seeing him—which she wasn't. She just liked pastries. A lot.

"You sure you're okay?" he asked.

The question confused her. "About what?"

"About Tracksuit Guy."

Right. Tracksuit Guy. Felix was worried she had a stalker. Which it was kind of looking like she did, in one way or another. Somehow, she suspected the guy did actually know her. Or, at least, thought he did. And, truth be told, there was something about him that was vaguely familiar to her.

But who he really was? Who knew? Not Rory, that was for sure. The guy could be anybody. Her arch-nemesis. Or her brother. Or even her husband. She had absolutely no way of knowing, since she had absolutely no memory of her life prior to eight and a half months ago, when she woke up in a Gary, Indiana, hospital with her head swathed in bandages. She'd been told her memory would probably eventually return. So far, however, she hadn't experienced the merest glimmer of recollection.

It was why, whenever she was asked about herself by someone in her new hometown, she had to make up something outrageous on the fly that no one else had knowledge of, so she could fabricate details to her heart's content. To the fine folk of Endicott, she'd been everything from a fortune cookie writer to a surfing instructor. No way was she going to tell her new neighbors she had no idea who she really was. That was an excellent way to make sure she never fit in here. And she desperately wanted to fit in in Endicott. Not only was this town the gentlest, most peaceful, most stable place she could imagine, but she had nowhere else to go. Or maybe she did have somewhere to go. She just didn't know where it was or who populated it.

"I'm fine," she assured Felix.

She was sure whoever Tracksuit Guy was, he wasn't actually a stalker. At least not the way Felix thought he was. More was the pity. Because an actual stalker like that would have been way easier to deal with. An actual stalker could be taken care of by a call to the police. Tracksuit Guy, however? Well, how was Rory supposed to explain to the police that she couldn't know for sure who he was, because she didn't even know for sure who *she* was? Best just to keep her distance. From him and everyone else. Including Felix.

Especially Felix.

"I'm fine," she told him again.

"You're positive?"

"I'm positive."

It was a lie, of course. So was the part about her being fine. But she always lied when she was asked something like that. Rory wasn't positive of anything these days. And she certainly wasn't fine. She would never be either of those things again. Not unless her memory returned. Though there was a part of her that honestly hoped it didn't. Because something—she had no idea what—told her she might not want to know.

She looked toward her front windows again to see that Tracksuit Guy was still out there. And she found herself hoping her former life wasn't about to come knocking on her door.

Chapter Two

It was with much exhaustion that Rory crossed her back room Saturday evening, after locking up the front of her shop, to lock the alley entrance, too. What had promised to be a reasonably normal, fairly easy day had turned into one of pandemonium, with a last-minute order for wedding flowers—*wedding flowers*, which normally took weeks, or even months, of planning—when an Indianapolis florist's van was totaled in an accident on I-65, just north of Columbus. Fortunately, the driver was fine, but the flowers? Not so much. Even with Wallflowers's simple, everyday assortment of blooms, Rory and Ezra had managed to pull together some really beautiful arrangements in a matter of hours, and the bride, who also happened to be a member of one of Endicott's most prominent families, had been exceedingly pleased. Even better, so had her mother. No doubt Wallflowers would see some decent business in the future from both of them.

As usual, she was closing up her shop right around the time things at La Mariposa next door were just getting under way. She could hear the clatter of metal and glass coming from the open restaurant entrance as she pulled the shop door closed behind her. It was punctuated by the raucous mambo music Felix preferred in his kitchen—usually someone named Pérez Prado, she'd learned from one of the dishwashers. As she turned the key in the dead bolt, she heard someone shout for "More *lechon asada,* pronto," while someone else was missing a *croqueta* on their plate. Sounded like it was going to be a long night for the restaurant's chef.

She stretched one last time as she inhaled the delectable aroma from the restaurant. She really would have loved to eat there sometime. Or get something to carry out to eat at home. But that would have meant seeing more of Felix, so… So instead, she trudged up the metal stairs attached to the brick building that led to the second floor and unlocked the metal door at the top. On the other side was a narrow hallway that led to a roof access, a spacious stockroom, and a not-quite-spacious-enough apartment. But even though her place was small—only one bedroom, one bathroom, a living room and a kitchen—Rory didn't care. It and Wallflowers were the only things in the world that were *hers*.

At least, the only things she was confident were hers. For all she knew, she could be the owner of a vast estate somewhere, with millions of dollars in the bank. Or she could be homeless and penniless. Or anything in between. Even after the passage of nearly nine months since the accident that had landed her in a hospital, fighting for her life—the accident that probably hadn't been an accident at all—Rory still hadn't enjoyed even a glimmer of memory from her life beforehand.

After showering and changing into pajamas—a loose T-shirt with a cartoon TV kitten and cotton pants spattered with more cats—she retired to her bedroom with a dirty martini and a book about orchid smugglers. As she neared her bed, however, instead of climbing into it, she set her drink and book on the nightstand and crouched at the side. After a moment's hesitation, she withdrew a wide, shallow box from beneath it. Inside were the only things in the world she'd owned before buying her shop and apartment. The things that had been returned to her when she left the hospital in Gary, Indiana, eight months ago.

Seeing Tracksuit Guy today, and talking to Felix about him, had roused more of the recent memories she always did her best to tamp down—the first memories she had of her current life. Memories of a sterile hospital room, a doctor named Saddiq and a social worker named Min, and the worst hangover Rory had ever had. Though why she'd assumed it was a hangover at the time, she had no idea. That was just the first thing that popped into her aching head when she awoke and realized how much it hurt.

But when she reached up and felt a thick swath of bandaging there, she knew she had something far worse than a hangover. A three-inch-long gash across the top of her cranium, for one thing, she was told. Twelve staples in her head, for another. A nasty hematoma and cracked skull, too, just to add to the fun. Oh, and also a complete and utter loss of memory. The nurse told her she'd arrived at the hospital thirty-six hours earlier, unconscious in the back of an ambulance, with no ID. A couple of eyewitnesses had seen her being tossed out of a moving car and into a trio of trash cans before the vehicle sped off into the darkness. Her head had been sliced open by a broken bottle, the contusion and fracture a result of her head slamming onto the pavement.

And that was it. Everything Rory knew about what had happened to her late into the night last New Year's Eve. Hell of a way to start the New Year.

She looked at the box again and, after a small hesitation, lifted the lid. The contents were sparse, but they were telling. She removed a tiny leather miniskirt, a hot-pink lamé halter top, a chartreuse faux-fur jacket, two torn fishnet thigh-highs, and a single glittery platform shoe. No purse. No ID. No undergarments. In a word, yikes. Min, the social worker who had been assigned to her case, told Rory there were no indications that she'd been assaulted, which had been a small source of comfort, but still. Her attire that night didn't exactly speak to her being an upstanding pillar of the community.

There was a long, thick braid of hair in the box, too. They'd had to shave a good bit of her head to stitch her up, so after she left the hospital, Rory had gone to a salon to have the rest of it cut as short as she could tolerate, too, to even things up. Although her hair had grown back jet-black—and surprisingly quickly, too—her hair before had been dyed blond and liberally streaked with gold and amber. The woman she was today couldn't imagine wearing the clothes in the box or having hair as long and dazzling as the mass in her hand. But the woman she used to be had clearly lived a life that included both. Just who the hell had Rory been as recently as a year ago?

Weirdest of all the things that had been returned to her at the hospital, however, was the jewelry she'd been wearing that night—jewelry she no longer had. Not because they included giant gaudy earrings, bracelets, and a necklace, since the pieces had been as tacky as the rest of her attire. But because the jewelry she'd assumed was worthless hunks of junk made of glass and plated metal turned out to be anything but. The nurse who returned Rory's belongings to her at the end of her stay had been a fan of fine jewelry and suggested she get them appraised, just in case. When Rory had, she'd been stunned to discover the stones, as big and garish as they were, were real. And the metal was pure gold. Her jewelry was worth a small fortune.

Enough to start a new life.

Which she eventually had, thanks to Min and some state agencies that eventually helped her find her way to Endicott. As Min had gone through a list of potential jobs and small businesses that might interest her, Rory had been immediately drawn to a small flower shop in southern Indiana whose owner wanted to retire and move to Florida. She had no idea how she knew, but she was certain she knew flowers and how to sell them. And then, the moment she set foot in Endicott, she'd been enchanted by the little town where everyone told her hello, even without knowing who she was. And the moment she stepped into Wallflowers…

She had no idea why she found the place so inviting, so familiar. Nor did she understand how she knew the name of every flower and plant that was available for sale. Or why looking at them instantly launched visions in her mind of arranging them in ways that were absolutely beautiful. So what could she do but make an offer on the place?

Her knowledge of floristry, however, seemed to be the only real knowledge she did have. She certainly discovered quickly that she knew little to nothing about running a business. As a result, even a month after opening, she was barely keeping her head above water. She was reading books and watching online tutorials about running a retail establishment, but it was still a challenge.

She'd get there, though, she told herself. Hey, look how far she'd come in just eight months. Maybe she didn't know her real name or have any idea who she really was, but, by god, she'd survived a near-death experience and was rebuilding her life from scratch. She just wished—

Well. She wished for a lot of things. Strangely, however, one of them wasn't knowing who she really was. Not when she looked at the only remnants she had of her past. Who knew what kind of person she used to be? At this point, she just wanted to live the best life she could from here on out. Certainly better than the one she evidently left behind.

Hastily, she tucked everything that had come out of the box back into it. She ought to just get rid of it. Toss it all in the dumpster behind her shop. Something about doing that felt wrong, though. As if she were throwing away a part of herself, however unsavory it seemed. So she closed the box and shoved it back under the bed and told herself to forget about everything in it. The same way she'd forgotten everything else about herself.

She stood and was about to climb into bed when her doorbell rang—the bell on the outer door in the alley, at the top of the metal stairs. She glanced at the clock on her nightstand. It was just past eleven. Who would be ringing her bell this time of night? With a knot in her stomach, she grabbed her phone from the table where she'd left it and checked her doorbell camera. Felix. Felix

Suarez was at her door at eleven o'clock at night. Even for him, this was intrusive.

But instead of telling him to shove off, she made her way to her apartment door, then the outer door, to open it. He was still wearing his chef clothes, but where they'd been pristine this morning, they were now spattered with reds, browns and greens. And he reeked of onions and cumin. Not that she minded that last part, because he smelled like his restaurant, and his restaurant always smelled incredible. Truth be told, she kind of didn't mind the disheveled chef's jacket, either, because he'd undone the top few buttons, and it hung open just enough to reveal a naked collar-bone and the merest hint of what promised to be a truly spectacular pectoral muscle. A small gold cross winked at the top of his sternum. The delicious clavicle and pecs didn't surprise her, but the cross did. Felix was one of the most irreverent people she'd ever met.

Then she remembered she only had eight and a half months' worth of memory when it came to meeting people. Which meant there was no question that Felix was, hands down, *the* most irreverent person she'd ever met.

He grinned. Irreverently. "Glad you're still up."

"What would you have done if I hadn't been?"

"I would've rung the bell again."

She expelled a restless sound. She didn't doubt it for a minute.

He lifted a box she hadn't noticed he was carrying because, well, naked collarbone and pecs. She recognized it as one of La Mariposa's to-go boxes.

"I brought you a present," he told her. "The new pastelitos Arjun made this morning. Sorry I didn't make it over after the brunch rush. Which became the lunch rush. Which became the dinner rush. We just now closed the kitchen."

Which meant Felix had put in a roughly fourteen-hour day. The man had some work ethic, she'd give him that.

"You should be in bed," she told him.

Belatedly, she realized how easily that statement could be misconstrued as a double entendre. She realized it because Felix's grin immediately went from irreverent to lascivious.

"If that's an invitation..." he said.

She immediately shook her head. Not to put too fine a point on it, but, "It is not," she told him. She took the box of pastelitos from him. "This was nice of you. Thank you. I owe you."

He shrugged. *"Hoy por ti, mañana por mí."*

The comment brought Rory up short. Mostly because she understood it, even though it was spoken in Spanish, a language she didn't know she understood. "Today for you, tomorrow for me," she translated.

Felix smiled again. "Eh, way to go, *yuma.* I didn't know you spoke Spanish."

Before she could stop herself, Rory replied, "Neither did I."

Felix's smile fell, and he narrowed his eyes. "How can you not know what you know?"

"That came out wrong," she said. "I meant..." What had she meant? And how did she know what Felix had meant just a minute ago? She shook her head, as if she were physically trying to clear it of her confusion. But she was still massively confused.

"Say it again," she told him.

Now he looked confused, too. But he repeated, *"Hoy por ti, mañana por mí."*

Rory knew she'd heard that phrase somewhere before. Maybe not spoken exactly the way Felix had, but 99 percent that way. Weirdly, though, she was pretty sure she'd heard it spoken by a woman. What woman? She had no idea.

Felix continued speaking, completely in Spanish, as if she would understand every word he said. But she didn't understand any of it. She caught one or two words that she thought she might recognize, but the gist of his monologue went right over her head.

"Stop!" she finally told him. "I don't understand." Then, surprising herself again, she told him, *"No comprendo."*

He smiled again. "You understand something, *mija*."

Mija. She understood that, too. It was a term of endearment. Someone had called her that at some point in her life. Rory *knew* it. She didn't know how she knew it, but she did. Again, however, she thought it had been a woman who called her that.

"I—" she began. But she had no idea what else to say. Her brain, however, evidently did. "Do you want to come in for a drink?" she heard herself ask. And even though, normally, the last thing she would do was invite someone—especially Felix Suarez—into her home late at night when she was in her pajamas, she couldn't deny that, at the moment, she really, really wanted to talk to him.

"There's nothing I would love more," Felix told her before she had a chance to change her mind.

Then, just to be sure, he pushed past her and through the door. When he did, he brushed against her, enveloping her in both the delicious aroma of his restaurant and the heat and potency that was inherently him. Instinctively, Rory took a step backward, nearly dropping the boxed pastries and tripping over her own feet. But Felix intercepted, catching both her and her treats, curling an arm absently around her waist and leading her into her apartment.

Once inside, she immediately pulled out of his grasp and escaped to her kitchen, setting his gift on the countertop and doing her best to quell the fire coursing through every place on her body Felix had touched. Quieting the racing of her heart, however, was another matter, because it just kept on pounding.

"Um, I left my drink in the bedroom," she told him. "Be right back." 'Cause, suddenly, she really needed that martini.

Hastily, she retrieved it, downing it in its entirety by the time she returned to the kitchen. She found Felix leaning against her counter between the sink and the fridge, his arms open, gripping the countertop with both hands, his feet crossed at the ankles. He was the picture of confidence and serenity, two states of mind Rory desperately wished she could command for herself. Unfortunately, as long as she had Felix in her apartment, she doubted she would be able to achieve either. What had she been thinking to invite him in?

Oh, right. That he might have some kind of mystical key to unlocking her memory, since the phrase he'd uttered was the first thing that had seemed familiar to her since her injury.

She inhaled a deep breath and headed for the fridge, wishing it opened from the other side, since that would put at least a little distance between her and Felix.

"What'll you have?" she asked as she opened the freezer to extract the cocktail shaker that still held another serving of her own drink.

"What are you having?" he asked.

"Dirty martini."

He wrinkled his nose in distaste. "Really? You don't seem the dirty-martini type."

She didn't? "I don't?" she asked before she could stop herself.

He shook his head.

"What's the dirty-martini type?"

He shrugged. "Not you."

She wanted to ask him to elaborate, but was afraid of what he might say. Like maybe that the dirty-martini type wore leather miniskirts and hot-pink lamé halter tops and had a job where she, ah, worked nights.

She shrugged, too, as she shook the metal mixer. "Well, I don't mind them."

"Don't mind them," he echoed. "That's not exactly a ringing endorsement. You should let me make you a mojito sometime. Now, *that's* a refreshing cocktail."

Okay, so maybe dirty martinis weren't her

favorite thing. They were a familiar thing, and Rory had precious few of those in her life. The day she'd been sprung from the hospital, she and Min had gone out for a celebratory drink, and when the bartender asked her what she was having, "dirty martini" was what popped out of her mouth. The minute she sipped it, the taste was familiar, and she knew it was her regular order in a bar, even if it wasn't the most delicious thing she'd ever had. Once she was settled in her own place, when she went to make one for herself, she knew exactly how to do it. Who knew how she knew? Not Rory, that was for sure. But it was familiar. So for that reason, if no other, it was her favorite drink.

She told Felix, "I also have some Scotch and some cognac."

She'd bought those when she bought the martini fixings, because somehow they all went together in her head. She didn't know who in her life liked Scotch or cognac, but evidently, someone did, if she'd been so inclined to include them in her purchase.

"No beer?" Felix asked.

She shook her head. She didn't like beer. Amnesia was weird for a variety of reasons, not the least of which was knowing what she did and didn't like, even though she may not have even sampled the things she knew she did and didn't like since returning to the land of the living. There may have even been pretty major reasons for her preferences, but she didn't know what they were, either.

"Cognac is fine," he told her.

When she retrieved the bottle from the cabinet that held her meager bar, Felix immediately noted the brand and raised his eyebrows.

"Wow, that's the good stuff," he said. "You have excellent taste." He checked out the other labels in the cabinet, then looked back at Rory with much interest. "Very good taste. Very expensive taste."

He was right. The liquor had cost more than she would have liked to spend. But when she was making purchases to stock her kitchen, she realized she knew all the brands she liked for just about anything she could consume. None of it had come cheap. But all the other labels might as well have been written in Greek, for what she knew about them. She'd been so happy to see something she was sure about—even if she didn't know how she was sure—that she hadn't minded spending the extra money. Besides, it wasn't like she was going to have any kind of social life she needed to budget for.

She poured a generous amount of the cognac

into a glass and handed it to him, then refilled her own. For a moment, they only stood silently in the kitchen, looking at each other, as if neither knew exactly what to say. And Rory realized in that moment that a person could drown in the golden depths of Felix Suarez's eyes.

Finally, Rory told him, "Um, have a seat," gesturing toward her living room.

The only option, she realized belatedly, was a not particularly large sofa. See above comment about not having any kind of social life to budget for. Having coffee and end tables had seemed more practical.

She didn't have to tell him twice. Felix happily made his way to the sofa and sat down. Rory followed, resigned to her fate and with a note-to-self that she should be a lot more careful in the future about who she invited into her home. Even so, she really did want to talk more to Felix. Needed to talk more to Felix. Somehow she understood some Spanish from her previous life. He was her only key to learning more about that at the moment.

"So..." she began.

Felix looked super interested in how she was going to finish that opening.

She decided she might as well just cut to the chase. "Could you say something else in Spanish?"

It clearly wasn't the finish he'd been hoping for. "I'm sorry?" he said.

"Say something else in Spanish," she repeated.

He gazed at her in confusion for a moment, then said something in Spanish that she didn't understand a word of. Damn.

"What did you just say?" she asked.

"You didn't understand it?"

She shook her head.

"I said you're acting very strange tonight."

She sipped her drink, mostly to keep herself from saying something snarky in reply, which was her first instinct. She couldn't afford to alienate Felix right now. "Then, clearly, no one has ever told me I act strange," she said. "Say something else."

Again, he said something she didn't recognize, but thanks to his inflection at the end, she knew it was a question.

"I didn't get that, either," she told him. "What did you ask me?"

He grinned. "I asked how much you've had to drink tonight."

"This is only my second," she assured him.

He didn't look like he believed her. Fine.

"Okay, this time, try something common," she told him.

He made a face at her, then said, *"¿Cómo estás?"*

She made a face back. "Something I wouldn't

learn in first-grade Spanish. Like some kind of well-known saying. The way *Hoy por ti, mañana por mí* is."

He sighed with much exasperation. "Okay. One of my grandmother's favorites. Whenever I came home late as a teenager, smelling of things she didn't think I should be smelling of, Tita would tell me, *Dime con quién andas, y te diré quién eres.*"

Rory emitted an involuntary squeal of delight. "Tell me who you run around with, and I'll tell you who you are," she translated.

"Close enough," Felix said. "So why do you only understand Spanish if it's some kind of worn-out platitude?"

She shook her head. "I don't know."

"How can you not know?" he asked. "That's crazy."

She bristled at the comment. She wasn't crazy. She had retrograde or traumatic amnesia resulting from a head injury. Or, possibly, dissociative or psychogenic amnesia caused by some kind of major psychological trauma. Though Dr. Saddiq had told her that last scenario was unlikely. Only time would tell for sure. Provided she eventually regained her memory. But she for sure wasn't crazy.

At least, she didn't think so.

Even so, amnesia wasn't exactly the sort of thing most people ran into in their everyday lives.

It was the stuff of daytime dramas and detective thrillers. So maybe in that sense it was a little… out of the ordinary.

Felix was still looking at her as if he needed a response for his question. She wished she could give him one. One that was honest and made sense. Maybe if she—

She halted the thought before it could even form in her brain. No, she could not confide in Felix. She could not tell him anything about her condition. She'd come to Endicott to start life over. Not just because she had no idea what her previous life had been like, but because there was a part of her that honestly wasn't sure she wanted to find out. The part of her that did want to find out, though, realized doing so meant uncovering things about herself that might be less than savory. Deep down, Rory wanted—and needed—to find out who she really was. Felix was the first person she'd encountered who'd offered her some kind of insight, however small, into who that might be. There was a chance he could help her more. Even if he was the last sort of person she would normally ever choose to confide in.

She chuckled inwardly at that. She had no idea who the real Rory Vincent—whose name wasn't even Rory Vincent—would choose to confide in.

For all she knew, Felix was exactly the kind of person she'd run around with in her previous life.

She enjoyed another swallow of her drink. Maybe it was the hastily consumed martinis. Maybe it was the sheer giddiness of finally having something in her current life offer her a clue as to who she might have been in her past. Or, hell, maybe it was just the way Felix was looking at her—as if he were genuinely concerned about her welfare and wanted to help her in any way he could. Maybe it was all of the above. Rory only knew that, after eight and a half months of hiding who she was—of not even knowing who she was—she finally had an opportunity to confide in someone. Maybe Felix wasn't the best candidate to bare her soul to, but right now, he was all she had.

"Felix," she said, "can I confess something to you about myself? Something kind of strange? But really important? And, if I do, do you promise not to tell anyone in Endicott? Do you promise to keep it a secret between just you and me? 'Cause I could really use some help."

Chapter Three

Felix looked at Rory and wondered just what the hell was going on. This night was not turning out the way he'd thought it would. He'd figured he'd bring the pastelitos up to her, she'd throw him some half-baked thanks and close the door in his face, then he'd go back to his place and spend the night fantasizing about how differently things could have turned out. But this? This was just weird.

Okay, yeah, he'd had a long day at the restaurant—and an even longer night—but that was nothing new. It shouldn't be messing with his head the way his head was being messed with at the moment. He'd been surprised when Rory invited him in for a drink, but thought maybe she was doing it as a way to say thanks for the pastelitos. Or, hey, maybe even because she wanted to get to know him better. It could happen. But no. She'd just wanted some kind of freaky Spanish lesson that made his head spin even more. And now she was asking if she could let him in on some kind of secret that he wasn't supposed to tell anyone?

Bizarro, acere. Muy bizarro.

"A strange confession about yourself?" he echoed. "*Mija*, what could be strange about you? You're as straight as they come. I've never met anyone as upright and do-right as you."

He thought she'd take his words as a compliment. Or, at the very least, in agreement. She really was as upright and do-right as they came. Instead, her expression changed to one of distress.

"You don't know anything about me," she told him.

"I know you don't tolerate any nonsense," he said. "I know you keep to yourself. I know you live modestly. I know you treat your workers well. And I know you run your business the way I run mine—like it's the only thing you have in the world. That's pretty much all I need to know about a person."

She looked like she didn't believe him.

So he continued, "Okay, if what the Endicott grapevine has to say can be believed, I also know you've done some really amazing things with your life. I'm still trying to figure out how you landed here instead of in some major city with some kind of job that's full of challenge and adventure."

Halfway through what he was saying, she closed her eyes and, so imperceptibly that he almost didn't notice it, shook her head. "And what if the Endicott grapevine can't be believed?" she asked.

Well, that was just crazy talk. The gossipers of Endicott might be busybodies, but they were almost never wrong. If Ivy Clutterbuck told Felix that she heard Rory Vincent used to be a professional panda nanny, then by god, there was no reason to believe Rory hadn't been a professional panda nanny.

Still, he'd indulge her. "So what if they can't?"

"What about a person's past?" she asked.

"What about it?"

"Don't you think a person's past is important?"

Felix shook his head. "Only considering that a person's past has made them what they are today."

She uttered a sound of…something…at that. He wasn't sure what. Not derision. Not relief. Not anything he could put his finger on. But it suggested she put a lot more emphasis on a person's past than he did.

Felix was adamant. "And what a person is today is what's important." Of that, if nothing else in this world, he was sure. No one was without their mistakes or regrets. No one. And he didn't fault anyone for those.

"What if a person doesn't have a past?" Rory asked.

It was an odd question. But then, this whole evening was turning out odd. "Everybody has a past, Rory."

Now her expression was clear. She was obviously distraught. "Not me," she said.

"*Mija*, seriously, how much have you had to drink tonight?"

She chuckled at that, but there was nothing happy in the sound. She held up her glass. "This really is only my second. I might be a little buzzed, but I'm not drunk."

That remained to be seen. He sighed. "Okay, fine. Tell me this deep, dark secret about yourself." Which was probably going to end up being something like she totally believed some conspiracy theory about how genetically altered dung beetles were infiltrating the highest levels of government, in which case, the joke was on her, because everyone in the country already knew that was true.

She started to lift her drink to her mouth again, then seemed to remember his admonition about whether or not she was drunk and set it resolutely on the coffee table. She met his gaze levelly. Barely two feet separated them on the couch. He was close enough to see that her eyes weren't quite as dark as he first thought. There were little flecks of copper surrounding her pupils like tiny starbursts.

"About nine months ago," she said, "I was involved in an accident."

"A car accident?"

"Kind of."

"How can it just be 'kind of' a car accident?"

She hesitated only a moment before clarifying, "I was sort of…thrown out of a moving car."

Felix's eyebrows shot up at that. He couldn't help it. Who would throw someone out of a moving car? Especially someone like Rory, who was a perfectly nice woman. Usually.

"Who threw you out of a car?" he asked.

"I don't know," she told him.

"What, did you have a bag over your head? Were you being kidnapped?"

He'd meant the questions as a joke. Unfortunately, judging by her expression, both of those things were possibilities.

"Rory?" he prodded, starting to feel a little alarmed.

But she just shook her head. "I don't know. I mean, I didn't have a bag over my head when they found me, but I have no idea about the kidnapping part."

Felix covered his mouth with one hand. Mostly to keep himself from voicing any of the million things shooting through his head at the moment. Rory, however, seemed to have gotten over her reticence, because she quickly continued.

"It happened on New Year's Eve. I don't remember anything about that night. Or anything that happened before it. I just remember waking up in the hospital afterward."

Felix dropped his hand back to his lap, but he still had no idea what to say. Mostly because the word that referred to the condition Rory was describing was a word that, in his experience, had only cropped up in ridiculous scenarios created by novelists and screenwriters who seemed to have run out of ideas.

"I have amnesia, Felix."

Not that that was going to stop Rory from saying the word aloud anyway. Not that he had any idea how to respond.

"Probably retrograde or traumatic amnesia, thanks to the head injury," she continued. "Which means there's a decent chance my memories will eventually return."

Felix sensed a *But*...coming.

"But," she said, "there's a chance it could be something called dissociative or psychogenic amnesia."

Not that he was sure he wanted to know the answer, but he asked anyway. "Which means?"

"Which means it could be the result of something that happened to me that was so terrible, my mind has blocked out it and everything leading up to it."

"So...your entire life?"

Her look of distress turned to one akin to fear. "Yeah, maybe."

Felix leaned back on the sofa, his gaze never leaving hers. Had he thought the evening was weird? Wow, he'd been so wrong about that. This went way, *way* beyond weird.

"You don't remember anything from before New Year's Eve?" he asked. "Nothing at all?"

She shook her head. "Nothing has been concretely familiar to me until tonight. Not until you said those things in Spanish that I understood. Those were more than familiar, Felix. I knew those phrases. I knew someone had said them to me before. Not just an impression of it. Knowledge. They're the first things in nearly nine months that I have *known*. Not just been familiar with. *Known*. I just don't know how or why, but I can't stress enough how huge that is for me."

"How do you know your name is Rory Vincent?" he asked.

"That's not my name," she told him. "I don't know my real name. Rory Vincent is something that came to mind after an occupational therapist coaxed it out of me, but I don't know why or what it means."

Felix did his best to wrap his head around everything she was saying. "How do you know it's not your real name?"

"Min—she's the social worker who was assigned to me at the hospital to help me get through everything—tried to find someone with that name who fit my description, but there wasn't anyone."

"So you didn't even have any ID on you when you..." He hesitated. It wasn't like it was every day that you asked someone about how they were thrown out of a car.

She shook her head. "Just the clothes on my back."

"But you bought your shop," he pointed out. "I assume you pay taxes. How can you do that without an identity?"

"Through the kindness of strangers and social services," she said. "Since January, I've gotten a lot of help from state agencies that relocated me here from Gary, which is where my accident happened."

That surprised Felix even more. Not only was Gary clear on the other side of the state, it was the antithesis of Endicott in every other way, too. It was probably nearly ten times the population, for one thing. Not to mention high in crime and poverty, which were pretty much nonexistent here. Quality of life, which Endicott had in abundance, was pretty low there. If that was where Rory was originally from, chances were good she hadn't had an easy time of it prior to losing her memory. Maybe she had a point about the trauma thing.

"So if you only had the clothes on your back," he said, "that has to mean you didn't have any money, right? How did you swing the purchase of the shop?"

Now she looked a little uncomfortable. "When I said 'the clothes on my back,' that included the accessories in my ears and around my neck and wrists."

Felix eyed her in confusion.

"Jewelry," she told him. "I was wearing a lot of jewelry that turned out to be super valuable."

He didn't think it was possible for her story to get any weirder, but there it went. "Then you might be from a wealthy family," he said. "And a wealthy family would be looking for a missing member."

She looked even more uncomfortable now. "Not necessarily," she said. But she didn't elaborate.

He started to ask her how she could know that, but she hurried on, saying, "I was able to sell it for quite a bit of money. Enough for a good down payment on Wallflowers. Min helped me with everything else—the Realtor, the bank, anything else that involved paperwork or record keeping."

Felix's head was starting to spin. Rory seemed to recognize his state of confusion. Quickly, she filled him in on as many details as she could about what happened to her on New Year's Eve. About waking up in a hospital not knowing who she was or where she was from or whether or not she had any family. About how all efforts to locate anyone who could identify her were fruitless. About how, over the next few months, she saw doctors and mental health experts and therapists of every stripe. About how nothing had helped her regain even a sliver of her memory. About how she finally ended up in Endicott. By the end of her story, he was feeling a little less confused, but way more uneasy.

"Okay, let me get this straight," he said when she finally stopped talking. "You have no memory of your life before last New Year's Eve, but somehow, you realize the things you like, like food and music and books."

She nodded. "But only if you catch me off guard and ask me point-blank what I want before I have a chance to think about it. Or if I hear or see something that's a specific trigger. Like when I saw *To Kill a Mockingbird* in the window of Barton's Bookstore and remembered the story enough to know I'd read it. Or when I heard Lizzo on the radio singing 'Juice,' I could jump right in and sing along because I already knew the lyrics."

"So you know the *kind* of person you are. You just don't know who you *actually* are."

Her expression grew distressed again. "No, I don't know where I'm from or how old I am or whether or not I have any family or…or anything like that. But the thing is, Felix, I actually don't know what *kind* of person I am, either."

"That's ridiculous," he said. "Of course you know what kind of person you are. I mean, you are what you are, right?"

"Maybe?" she said uncertainly. "But I don't know what kind of person I used to be. And that scares me, too."

He wanted to argue that a person didn't change who they were just because they hit their head or lost their memory. Somebody who was nice would still be nice, even if they couldn't remember who they were. Then again, he supposed a person's values and morals were a result of the way they grew up, and if she couldn't remember the way she grew up, maybe, in a way, she had a point.

Gah. This was all so incredible. He couldn't believe he was having this conversation.

Then another thought struck him. She'd said there was a good chance her memories would eventually return. But what if they didn't? In fact, what if they got even worse? Head injuries were nothing to take lightly. What if there came a time when Rory didn't remember the here and now? What if, someday, she forgot about Endicott? What if, someday, she forgot about him?

Fire exploded in his belly at the thought, and his mind began to reel. Nausea followed, then a loud buzzing erupted in his ears. His heart began to race, his chest grew constricted, and he felt hot all over. He jumped up from the sofa.

"I gotta go," he said suddenly.

Because if he didn't get out of there *now*, he was going to start panicking. Hard.

"What? No," Rory protested. She stood, too. "I have more questions I need to ask you."

Felix shook his head. "Not tonight. Sorry, Rory. But I gotta go. Now."

"But—"

Her remonstrations followed him all the way

to her front door. Even when he closed it behind himself, he could still hear her on the other side begging him to stay. But there was no way he was going to do that. Hell, as far as he was concerned in that moment, he never wanted to see Rory again. Yeah, maybe it was a harsh reaction to what she'd revealed to him tonight, but he had his reasons. Really good ones, too.

He didn't stop moving until he was safely ensconced in his own apartment, bolting first the outside door, then the inner one behind himself. Nestor, his grandmother's white cat, who had adored her when she was alive but had always shunned Felix as if he didn't exist, ran down the hall to greet him...until he saw that it was Felix and not his human, Marisol, *again*, then turned to retreat to wherever it was he normally disappeared. Nestor still didn't seem to understand that Tita wasn't coming back to the apartment, and he nightly made Felix aware that he would never measure up to the woman who had rescued him from a storm drain five years ago, when he was an abandoned kitten. Even though it was Felix who fed him now and made sure his favorite pillow was still on Tita's bed, and always left a window open for him to spy on the neighborhood as long as the weather was agreeable.

Nestor's rejection had gone on nightly for the

past two years, and every time it happened, it reminded Felix of the loss of his grandmother all over again. It was reason number forty-two why he was determined to never care about a person that much again.

On automatic pilot, he shed his dirty clothes and tossed them into the hamper, then showered and donned his usual nightwear of cotton pajama pants and nada else. Then he went to the kitchen for a much-needed beer, since he'd left his cognac at Rory's mostly untouched.

But when he grabbed the fridge door handle, he stopped before opening it. He hadn't changed anything in the apartment since Tita died, and a swirl of photographs she'd magnetted to the fridge since his childhood were still firmly in place. He'd barely paid attention to them over time, but tonight, one in the center immediately caught his attention. It was a photo from the summer when he was seven years old, taken at Endicott's only public pool. A photo of him and a half-dozen friends, including his two best—Chance and Max. Okay, his two *surviving* best friends. Because seated immediately to Felix's right, with her arm draped around his shoulder and his around hers, was another best friend he'd had once upon a time: Megan Campbell. Two summers after the photo was taken, she would be dead.

In between, Felix had watched her succumb to a rare childhood illness not unlike Alzheimer's. Her mother had worked as a hostess at La Mariposa, and Megan and Felix had spent a lot of time together on the weekends and evenings when her mother had a shift. And even when her mother wasn't working. Megan had been his first crush, before he was even old enough to know what a crush was. To watch her slowly decline to a disease he was also too young to understand had been heartbreaking. Especially when there came a time when she didn't recognize him and had no idea who he was and couldn't remember the times the two of them had shared together.

Reason number one why he was determined to never care about a person that much again.

Gently, he removed the photo from the refrigerator door. He continued to look at it as he retrieved a beer from inside and opened it. He told himself that Rory's amnesia and Megan's illness had nothing in common, other than the loss of memory. Megan's loss had been permanent. Her illness had been fatal. With time, there was a good chance Rory could recover her past. And there was nothing about amnesia that would kill her. There was no reason for him to not help her figure out who she was if he could.

A memory flashed in his head of going to

visit Megan not long before her death. His grandmother had warned him she wasn't doing very well and that maybe Felix shouldn't bother her or her family right now. But it had been more than a month since he'd seen her, and he missed her. Before going to her house, he went to the park and picked two big handfuls of her favorite flower. He didn't know what they were called, only that they were pale blue and star-shaped, with a yellow center. Max would tell him later, the day he and Felix encountered them again, when Felix was stomping them into the dirt, that they were wild hyacinth, and *Yo, Felix, knock it off, wild hyacinth never hurt anybody.* But that day, before going to see Megan, he brought them home and wrapped their stems in a wet paper towel surrounded by aluminum foil to keep them fresh. Then he'd headed over to see Megan.

Who gave him one look and cried out in distress because she didn't know who he was or how he'd gotten into her house. Then she'd pelted him with everything in her room she could grab, including a bedside lamp, which shattered against the wall behind him. He'd tried to comfort her, tried to remind her who he was. He'd tried to give her a hug. But she'd flailed and screamed and pushed him away. She'd been so terrified that she'd even grabbed a shard of the broken lamp and lunged at him, leaving a gash on his hand that had required three stitches.

Her father had come to her room and hurriedly escorted Felix away and, upon seeing his injury, had taken him to the hospital. On the way, he'd tried to explain why Megan had done what she had, but nine-year-old Felix had been as terrified by the experience as Megan had been, and he hadn't understood at all. Even now, decades later, when he did understand, the memory of that day shook him to his core.

He looked down at that hand now. He still had a scar there, even after two decades. Of course, that wasn't the only scar Megan had left on him. It was just the only one that showed.

Yeah, there was no reason for him not to help Rory. Except for the fact that there was no way he was *ever* going to revisit that part of his childhood again. And somehow, helping Rory, he knew, would put him right back in the thick of that time again.

He went to the trash can in the kitchen and stepped on the pedal to open its lid. For one long moment, he held the photo of him and Megan and their friends over it. They all looked so happy in the pic. Chance was behind them, doing rabbit ears over both of their heads, and Max was on

Felix's other side, making the kind of goofy face that seven-year-olds loved to make.

He muttered an epithet under his breath and removed his foot from the pedal. The trash can lid slowly closed. Felix enjoyed another deep swallow of his beer and returned the photo to its place on the fridge door.

He really ought to clean this place up, he thought as he walked to his bedroom. It had been two years since his grandmother's death, and the apartment badly needed updating. The restaurant was only open for brunch on Sundays, and it was closed all day Monday to give everyone at least one day off a week—including him. Tomorrow, after work, Felix should just start sorting through everything and getting rid of the stuff he didn't need anymore. Yeah. That was what he should do. No use living in the past. Especially when he had his sights set so intently on the future. A future that would leave Endicott—and a lot of his not-so-fond memories of the town—firmly in the past.

Where they belonged.

Chapter Four

When Rory knocked on Felix's door Sunday afternoon, the way he had hers the night before, she honestly didn't expect him to answer. She knew he sometimes left the running of La Mariposa's Sunday brunch entirely to Tinima, so that he could have two days off in a row, and this morning had evidently been one of those—she hadn't heard the heavy clank of his exterior door closing the way she usually did when he left. What had surprised her was that she hadn't heard his door open at all today. Even when he didn't work on Sundays, he generally went out somewhere, often with his two best friends, whom she had only met in passing, but who she hadn't been able to help noticing were as Hollywood handsome as Felix was.

So she had hoped to catch him at home now, having spent her entire day so far doing something she almost never did—baking. She told herself it was because she wanted to return the favor of the pastelitos Felix had brought over last night. But she really just needed an excuse to see him again. Not only because she still wanted to see if he could maybe stir some more memories for her, but also to find out why he'd left so abruptly last night.

She understood the revelation of her amnesia had probably rattled him. He might not even believe she actually had it—and she wouldn't blame him for that. It wasn't every day that a person encountered an amnesiac. But speaking more to Felix truly did seem like the only avenue she had to regaining her memory. Not only had his words yesterday been the first thing to shake some memories out of her brain, they'd also spurred dreams last night unlike any she'd had since her accident. Dreams about wandering through a big house that seemed vaguely familiar. And about being a little girl again, sitting in the back seat of a big car, with a pink sequined backpack beside her and a big man at the wheel driving her to what she knew would be her school.

Upon waking, Rory had been afraid she would forget the dreams, so she quickly wrote them down. But the dreams had stayed with her, as clear as when she first had them. So what else could she do but make an effort to see Felix again? Even if talking to him more didn't rouse any immediate memories, the conversation might spawn more dreams. Baking something for him had seemed like the most logical quid pro quo. The only problem was, she didn't know if she knew how to bake. So she closed her eyes and waited to see if her brain would reveal some small snippet of the knowledge of things she'd had once upon a time. And after a few minutes, she had her answer.

Fig cookies.

Rory realized she knew how to make fig cookies. Which she couldn't help thinking was a really weird thing to know how to make. She didn't even need a recipe, because there was one she had memorized that tumbled to the forefront of her brain, right down to the nutmeg and brandy. She'd run to Shrader's Scrimp 'n' Save up the street for a few things she didn't have on hand—not the least of which were figs, something she was surprised to recall were one of her favorite things. She just hoped Felix liked them, too. She'd even donned a fresh pair of jeans and a button-up shirt spattered with tiny forget-me-nots for the occasion.

She knocked a third time on the door. No response. Again. With a surprising depth of disappointment, she began to turn away…then heard the faint scrape of a door on the other side opening, followed by the metallic rasp of the dead bolt on the outer one. Finally, Felix stood before her, looking as if he'd been hip deep in, well, filth.

His faded jeans were streaked with dust and dirt, as was his torso—which was bare, save for the luscious assortment of muscle and sinew rippling from the base of his delectable throat to that otherworldly masculine U-shape just below his waist. Revealed almost in its entirety, she was delighted to see, thanks to the way his jeans were about as low-riding as they could be without requiring an R-rating. Framing it all were arms corded with salient biceps and triceps and other bumps of flesh she didn't know the names of but certainly appreciated seeing. His hair hung wetly over his forehead, and he shoved it back with both hands, something that made *aaalll* those muscles dance and frolic. Rory had never found sweatiness much of a turn-on when it came to men—at least, she didn't think she had—but with Felix…

Um, yeah. Okay. She could see why some women found such a condition sexy.

Ahem.

"Hi," she said, the word coming out barely louder than a whisper.

"Morning," he said as moved his hands to his sides. Making all those muscles dance some more. *Day-um*.

Then he seemed to remember who he was talking to and how their conversation of the night before had gone, because he suddenly stiffened and moved his hands to his hips. Which only made the waistband of his pants dip lower, revealing even more of that transcendent flesh. In a word, *Yikes*.

Eyes, up, Rory! Eyes up!

"Not exactly morning," she told him, meeting his gaze. "It's after two."

He looked surprised. "Wow. Guess I've been working harder than I realized."

Doing what? she wondered. Building an aircraft carrier? Out of filth?

"I'm actually kind of surprised to find you home," she told him. "You're usually out with your friends on Sunday."

She mentally kicked herself for revealing that she'd noticed that much about him. But he didn't seem to pick up on her gaffe.

"Not today," he said. "Chance is meeting a

couple of kids he's inheriting, and Max is out looking for his high school crush that everyone says has come back to town for the comet festival. They're both gonna be busy for a while."

Rory decided not to delve too deeply into either situation. Instead, she extended the two dozen fig cookies she'd wrapped in a white cotton napkin. She figured if Felix didn't want them all, he could share them with his friends or coworkers.

"This time, I brought you a present," she said.

He eyed her warily. "You did?"

She nodded. "Fig cookies. To make up for last night. I'm sorry I dropped the bombshell of my amnesia on you the way I did. I was hoping maybe we could pick up today where we left off last night, only this time I promise to go slow."

Instead of agreeing to her proposal, he only asked, "You know how to make Italian fig cookies?"

"Well, I don't know if they're Italian or not, but they're absolutely fig cookies."

She extended the bundle to him. Gingerly, he accepted it.

"The only fig cookies I've ever heard of are Italian fig cookies," he said as he unwrapped the napkin from around the assortment. "They're kind of a thing. Yep, that's what these are," he added when he saw them. "Who taught you to make Italian fig cookies?"

"I have no idea," she said.

He snapped his head back up at that, clearly not happy to hear another reference to their conversation from the night before. "Right," he said crisply.

"Look, Felix," she began before he could shut her down again, "could we please finish talking about what we talked about last night?" Maybe if she didn't bring up the word *amnesia*, he wouldn't spook so badly.

"We did finish," he said decisively.

"No, *you* finished. I still have a few things I'd like to talk to you about."

He was shaking his head before she even formed a full sentence. "Then talk about them with someone else."

"I don't have anyone else to talk to. In case you didn't notice, I haven't lived in Endicott long enough to make many friends."

She was afraid he would reply with something along the lines of *Including me*, since—all right, all right—she hadn't exactly been friendly with Felix before now. It was nothing personal. She hadn't been friendly with anyone. She couldn't afford to get to know anyone too well. She couldn't have people asking her questions about herself that she didn't have the answers to.

"I'm sorry," she said. "But if you'll just—"

"Thanks for the cookies," he interjected. He began wrapping them up again as he took a step back inside.

"Felix, wait," she pleaded. "If you'll just let me—"

"I'm sure they're delicious."

"But—"

He was about to close the door in her face—something she'd thought about doing to him the night before, she reminded herself ruefully. In desperation, she leaped forward, intending to insinuate herself between the door and the jamb. Instead, she insinuated herself between the jamb and Felix, just as he pulled the door closed on both of them. As a result, she was left squished between the jamb and him. Him and all that glorious naked, sweaty flesh. Which smelled like sage and sandalwood, she couldn't help noticing, along with the muskiness of his labor, which should have been a turnoff, yet was somehow anything but.

She waited for him to take another step backward. But he didn't. Instead, he just stayed pressed against her, his heat mingling with hers, the dewiness of his skin dampening hers, too. For one long moment, they only stood eye-to-eye and toe-to-toe, their breathing hitched as if by mutual accord. For one agonizing instant, Rory even thought Felix had begun to inch his head closer to hers. Without thinking, she lifted her free hand to his bare chest, tenting her fingers over his heart, feeling the heat of his flesh against her palm. It just felt like the most natural thing for her to do for some reason. Then he suddenly opened the door again, with enough force to nearly send it into the wall beside him, and took a giant step backward. After that, the spell was broken.

That didn't slow the rapid-fire beating of her heart, however. As long as Felix looked the way he did, and as long as she could remember the feel of his slick skin beneath her fingertips, she doubted anything was going to be able to assuage that.

"I'm kinda busy," he told her. But he made the comment halfheartedly, as if he really didn't mind so much being interrupted.

He was standing in the open door of his apartment proper now, and behind him, inside, she could see a jumble of boxes and items strewn about, almost as if he had just moved in and was trying to figure out where to put everything.

"Can I help?" she asked.

He wanted to say no, she could tell. But he

didn't exactly look happy about whatever he was doing. "Fine," he finally conceded. He stepped out of the way and slung the hand holding the cookie bundle toward the interior. "Come on in."

Rory rushed past him before he could change his mind. His apartment was bigger than hers, she noticed right away. His kitchen was larger, and he had an actual dining room, even if it was a bit small. And there was a hallway that led down to what looked like two bedrooms instead of her one. A white cat trotted out from somewhere to greet her, but stopped in his tracks when he saw it was a stranger. Then he fell back on his haunches to stare at her, his face almost comically obvious in its curiosity about her.

"You have a cat," she said, surprised. Felix didn't seem like the type to commit himself to the care and feeding of anyone, including a pet.

"My grandmother had a cat," he said, correcting her. "Nestor just tolerates me because he knows he can't evict me."

She smiled at that. "He sure is a handsome boy."

Rory dropped down on her haunches, too, mimicking the cat's posture. Immediately, Nestor stood and made his way over to her. When she extended a hand gingerly toward him, he stopped midstride. Then, with much suspicion, slowly made his way forward again. He sniffed her finger, then eyed her as if she were trying to fool him. After a moment, though, he gently placed his paw on her knee. She smiled and sat down on the floor, and he immediately crawled into her lap. And then, to her utter and absolute delight, he began to purr.

She looked up at Felix, who was gazing at her in something akin to awe. "I have never seen that cat warm up to someone. Ever. My grandmother was the only person he would give the time of day to. He barely speaks to me."

Rory smiled as a wave of almost-memory washed over her. "I think I have a cat."

"Oh, now, wait a minute," Felix said. "I mean, maybe Nestor and I aren't the best of friends, but you can't just swoop in here and claim him like that."

She laughed. "No, not Nestor. I think I have a cat in my other life. My real life."

His expression was deadpan. "What makes you think you own a cat?"

She looked down at Nestor again. "This feels very, very familiar. Like recently familiar. I think, wherever I normally live, I have a cat. I just hope someone is taking care of her in my absence."

Nestor settled more easily into her lap and purred louder.

"Her?" Felix echoed. "How do you know it's a girl cat?"

She shook her head. "I don't know how I know. I just know she is. And I'm pretty sure she's gray."

"Got a name?"

Rory closed her eyes and let her mind go blank. Gradually, an image of a gray cat in an open window swam into her mind's eye. The wall surrounding the window was painted bright blue—the kind of blue that showed up in photos of white homes in the Greek islands. There was a watercolor painting of a bright pink anemone to the right of the window, and she somehow knew she had painted it herself. But the cat she could see so clearly remained nameless.

She opened her eyes again. "No. No name. But I think I might know how to paint, too." *Note to self: Rory, visit Arabella's Art Supplies this afternoon.*

"Okay," Felix said, clearly a little baffled by the randomness of the statement.

Rory was baffled, too. This was the first time she'd ever experienced a concrete image of anything. And it had been so clear and colorful. For some reason, it gave her comfort. And it let her know, without question, that understanding those statements in Spanish from Felix last night had unlocked the first door in her brain that led to more memories. Now he had helped her unlock two. After almost nine months of knowing absolutely nothing about herself, she'd discovered two important things in a matter of hours. He really did seem to be the key to her recovery. She had to find a way to make sure she kept him close.

Nestor jumped up from her lap then and ambled over to an open window that overlooked the street below, jumping into it to survey his domain, looking very much like the cat she had just seen in her mind's eye. Rory stood and let her gaze wander around Felix's apartment again. The whole place really was a mess. He really did seem to be moving in. Or, she thought, with no small sense of panic, maybe moving out?

"Going somewhere?" she asked him.

He had moved into the kitchen to put the cookies on the counter, but spun around at her question—though not before she noticed that the muscles in his back were every bit as mouthwatering as ones on his front.

"What?"

"Are you moving?" she clarified. She gestured at the clutter. "It looks like you're packing to move out."

He followed her gaze and almost seemed surprised by the scene before him. "Oh. Yeah. I guess it kind of does." He looked at her again. "No, not packing to move out. Just getting rid of some stuff I should have boxed up after my grandmother died."

Rory had heard through the grapevine how La Mariposa had been started by Felix's grandmother, and how he'd taken the business over after her death. But she only knew the bare details. Not so much because she disliked gossip—on the contrary, she'd loved filling her empty brain with all this new information. But because having people talk about the comings and goings of their neighbors prevented Rory from having to talk about herself.

"Your grandmother came here from Cuba, right?" she asked.

He nodded, but smiled in a way that told her he knew she'd been indulging in the very gossip he probably didn't care for himself. At least, not when the subject matter was him.

"Sorry," she said. "I don't mean to pry. Mr. Kapileo told me."

Mr. Kapileo was her neighbor on the other side of Wallflowers, the owner of Kapileo's King Klothing, a big-and-tall store for men. This despite the fact that Mr. Kapileo himself was a half foot shorter than she. He was an excellent tailor, though. Even if he did have to use a stool most of the time.

"It's fine," Felix said. "I grew up here, don't forget. We call it the Endicott Telegraph for a reason.

It takes less than twenty minutes for everyone in town to know everyone else's backstory and business." He paused and eyed her thoughtfully. "Even you didn't escape. Might have taken longer than twenty minutes, since you're new here, but we've all heard about your accomplishments. I mean... Cirque de Soleil? Rhodes Scholar? Mount Kilimanjaro? Those are pretty major achievements."

Yeah, they were pretty major, Rory thought. Too bad they were big, fat lies. Had she realized how quickly news got around here in Endicott, she would have given herself a much more modest pedigree and stuck to it, regardless of who she was talking to. She just hadn't planned on being put on the spot the way she had been. She didn't think she'd ever lived in a small town before, because she'd been so taken aback by the interest in her as soon as she arrived. Everyone she'd encountered—from the elderly cashier at the Scrimp 'n' Save to the sk8er bois in the park—had wanted to know her entire life history the minute she said hello. But where she would have thought she would be put off by such intrusion, Rory had actually found it kind of nice. No one seemed like they were being nosy. They seemed genuinely interested to know who the newcomer in town was. So she'd felt an obligation to at least make herself seem interesting.

"Except," Felix said, "you can't remember anything about your life prior to New Year's Eve, so I guess none of that stuff is true, is it?"

Rory expelled a restless sound. "No. I'm sorry I lied to everyone. But I don't know the truth about myself. And it's kind of awkward to reply to someone's introduction with, 'Nice to meet you, too. I'm Rory. I have amnesia.'"

He looked uncomfortable again at her mention of the word. But he didn't recoil as badly as he had the night before. She still didn't know what to make of the harshness of that withdrawal.

"But you know flowers," he pointed out. "How do you know so much about being a florist? 'Cause you do seem to be good at that."

"Thanks. I have no idea. Maybe I used to have a shop like Wallflowers. Or maybe flower arrangement was a hobby of mine or something. I only know when Min was going over possible places for me to go and jobs I could line up, the minute she mentioned a florist for sale, I was totally interested. And when I saw the place, all this knowledge of plants and flowers and how to put them all together just sort of tumbled to the front of my brain, and I knew it would be perfect for me."

He didn't say anything more, so she returned to the subject of Felix, by way of his grandmother.

"So how long ago did your grandmother come to Endicott?"

She wanted to ask about his parents, too, but knew that was a taboo subject. Felix and his grandmother weren't the only Suarezes Rory had heard about. There had been stories about his mother, too, and how she'd been pregnant when she arrived in Endicott with Marisol but disappeared not long after his birth. *But you didn't hear that from me*, she'd been told by whoever said that. *Felix doesn't like to talk about his mother.*

Felix didn't look like he wanted to talk about his grandmother right now, either, but since the alternative was talking about her and her condition—something he obviously wanted to talk about even less—he replied, though with clear reluctance, "Tita and my grandfather left Cuba when things were heating up between Castro and Batista, before my mother was born."

"How did they wind up here? I mean, Endicott's great and all, but it's kind of a hidden treasure."

"Not every fifteen years, it's not," he pointed out.

Right. The comet thing. Rory had been more than a little surprised when the town started to get overrun with tourists not long after her arrival. Especially since so many of them were cosplaying as everything from ETs, to rocket ships, to entire solar systems. But she'd been enchanted by the stories her neighbors told her about the comet and all the myths and legends that had sprung up around him. Thanks to her amnesia, she'd never heard of Comet Bob before coming here. She kind of wondered if she would have heard of him before now, even without amnesia. He did seem to belong almost exclusively to the people of Endicott.

Not that she was complaining. Without the added tourist traffic, her shop would be struggling even more. And she and Ezra had been having fun with promotional deals on plants such as star jasmine, moonwort, Jupiter's beard, and cosmos.

"They settled in Miami when they first came to the States," Felix told her. "They opened a bodega on Calle Ocho, where they sold *Cubanos* and *chicharitas* and *batidos* and such."

"Which are...?"

He smiled for the first time since he'd opened the door to find her on the other side. "What? You don't know?"

She shook her head. "Guess whatever Spanish I learned, I didn't learn it from a Cuban. At least not one who cooks."

"Cubanos are pork sandwiches, chicharitas are plantain chips, and batidos are milkshakes. You'd know that if you ever came over to La Mariposa to eat."

Was that an invitation? she wondered. 'Cause that had sounded a bit like an invitation. And why did she kind of hope it was?

"So how did they end up here?" Rory asked, pushing the thought away. She was surprised to discover how much she was enjoying talking to Felix. She honestly didn't think she'd exchanged this many words with anyone in Endicott other than Ezra. And they only ever talked about flowers and the shop.

"They didn't," Felix said. "Not all of them, anyway. My grandfather died about six months before I was born. My grandmother moved up here with my mother to be closer to her sister, who was married to a farmer in Georgetown. Anyway, Tita and my mother started a catering business here in Endicott that eventually became La Mariposa, and then I was born, and a few months later, my mother took off, and we never saw her again. So...you want some lunch or something? I'm hungry."

As segues went, it wasn't the most graceful one in the world. But Rory knew better than to ask any more questions. In spite of her having shared with Felix parts of herself she hadn't shared with anyone else, the two of them really didn't know each other that well. And the way he'd glossed over his abandonment and gone straight to lunch made clear he was done talking about it.

"Sure," she said. "I'd love some lunch." Which was true, since the only thing she'd eaten since she woke up was a cup of coffee loaded with cream and sugar—the way she somehow knew she liked it—two figs, and one fig cookie, because she'd obviously had to do quality control and make sure they were good before bringing them over to Felix.

He looked grateful that she hadn't pursued the part about his mom taking off and never seeing her again. "Give me five minutes," he said. "I'll run downstairs and grab us whatever's left of the *revoltillo*." Before she could ask, he explained, "It's like an egg and sausage scramble, except with chayote, sweet peppers, and chorizo. You'll love it."

As he spoke, he grabbed a T-shirt hanging on the back of a dining room chair and tugged it over his head, then dashed out the door before she could say another word. She told herself he was not fleeing. He was just trying to get to the kitchen of La Mariposa before it closed. Except that he forgot to put on shoes, so yeah, okay, maybe he was fleeing. That was okay. She'd still be here when he got back.

Chapter Five

Felix cursed under his breath as he stood outside the back door of La Mariposa in his bare feet, waiting for Tinima to fill two to-go boxes with revoltillo and croquetas for his and Rory's lunch. Damn chefs de cuisine who played by the rules anyway. It was hardly likely the Indiana State Department of Health was going to pop into the restaurant and cite them all for his lack of footwear in the five minutes it would have taken him to fill the boxes himself. Then again, with the way his luck was going lately, he should have probably expected them.

"Here," Tinima said as she returned with two boxes.

Not for the first time, he wondered how she made it through an entire shift without getting so much as a butter spatter on her pristine white chef's jacket. The woman was a *ciguapa*, the Caribbean equivalent of a sorceress, he just knew it.

"I hope Rory enjoys it," she added with a smile as Felix took the boxes from her.

"I'm sure she wi— Hey, who said anything about Rory?" he said, hastily changing gears.

"You just did," Tinima said with a laugh. And a twinkle in her eye that Felix didn't much care for.

"It's not what you think," he told her.

"Of course it's not. I'm sure the two of you are just upstairs having a nice conversation about the weather."

Among other things. Things he really hadn't intended to reveal to her, like how his mother ran out on him shortly after he was born. Reason number two why he was determined to never care about a person that much again.

"Yeah, it's gonna be unseasonably warm for the next few days" he told Tinima as she turned back toward the kitchen, clearly having said all she needed to say. "We might want to put peach mojitos back on the menu!" he added to her retreating—and unlistening—form.

But Tinima was already off to plan other things. Probably his and Rory's wedding, since her promise to his grandmother on her deathbed had been that she'd make sure Felix found a nice woman and settled down.

Hah. Like that was going to happen to someone whose only interest in life was being a restaurateur. It especially wasn't going to happen here in Endicott. He knew every woman who lived here, and not one of them was anyone he could imagine spending the rest of his life with.

Immediately, Rory's face swam up to the forefront of his brain. *And not her, either, Tita*, he silently told his grandmother. No way was he going to get involved with someone who might never remember who she was and, for all he knew, could forget him, too.

He carried the boxes back upstairs, only to find Rory in his kitchen, washing dishes he'd left in the sink to wash himself later. And he couldn't help wondering if his grandmother was haunting him right at that very minute, showing him what a good catch Rory was, washing dishes she hadn't been asked to wash, dishes that didn't even belong to her, and couldn't he see how much happier he'd be with a nice girl like that to come home to every day?

He actually made a quick survey of the room to

see if there were any misty apparitions or glowing orbs floating around. Then he told himself he was being ridiculous.

"You don't have to do that," he told Rory as she set the last of the now-clean dishes in the rack to drain.

She spun around at the comment, but smiled. "I wanted to make myself useful. And I wasn't sure what you needed to pack."

He held up the boxes from the restaurant. "Lunch is ready. There's some Coco Rico in the fridge if you want to grab a couple," he added as he carried their meals to the table.

Rory joined him after retrieving two cans of the soda from his fridge, seating herself in the chair across from his just as Felix pushed one of the boxes toward her. She popped the tab of her drink with a satisfying hiss.

"What's Coco Rico?" she asked. "I've never seen it before."

"Says the woman whose memory is only nine months old," Felix replied.

"I know, but there are still brands I recognize," she told him. "When I go to the grocery store, I know what to buy, because I know I like it without having any memory of it. But this—" she pointed to the green and silver cans "—this I'm confident I've never seen before."

"It's like coconut soda. It's from Puerto Rico, but you can get it here. Well, not here in Endicott," he amended, "but there's a *supermercado* in Louisville that keeps it in stock. Tita used to buy it for me when I was a kid." He shrugged, a little embarrassed. "Some things you never outgrow, you know?"

He winced after saying it, realizing belatedly that, no, in fact, Rory had no way of knowing that herself, since she couldn't remember what she'd liked when she was a kid.

"It's okay, Felix," she assured him. "It's weird for me, too, even after living this way for nine months. Even I forget sometimes and say or think the wrong thing. I don't take any offense."

"Thanks," he told her.

As he popped the tab on his soda, Rory opened her box from the restaurant. When she did, she let out a cry of delighted surprise.

"Oh, this is beautiful," she said.

Felix took pride in his recipes and their presentation, but there was only so much you could do with what was essentially scrambled eggs with vegetables and a ham fritter. Yes, La Mariposa's revoltillo and croquetas looked delicious and delectable and tempting. But beautiful? That wasn't exactly a word he'd use to describe them.

Then he opened his own box and saw that

Tinima had garnished both meals with nasturtiums and violets and other edible flowers left over from the brunch salad specials, presumably to give them an added element of romance. Just what he needed. A matchmaking chef de cuisine. Well, that was just great.

On the other hand, the blossoms might impart an interesting flavor profile he hadn't considered before. Best not to be too hasty.

"Are all of La Mariposa's meals so pretty?" Rory asked.

Before he could stop himself, Felix said, to echo his earlier point, "You'd know that if you ever ate there. You should come in sometime."

Too late, he realized the statement could be interpreted as an invitation, however roundabout. As could his admonition of pretty much the same thing a little while ago. He quickly told himself it wasn't a problem, because no way would Rory ever accept an invitation from him of any kind. She'd made clear from day one that she intended to keep her distance from him and everyone in Endicott. The only reason she was having anything to do with him now was because she saw him as a means to an end and didn't feel like she had any choice.

So it surprised him when she told him, "I'd love to. Just tell me what day and what time."

Before, he would have jumped on her agreement and laid out exactly when and where, specifically tomorrow, since the restaurant was closed, and he could cook a meal for just the two of them. But that was before. Before he knew she was—there was no other way to say it—sick. Maybe amnesia wasn't a terminal disease the way Megan's illness had been, but then again, maybe it was. Even Rory hadn't been able to say there was a one-hundred-percent chance that her memory would return, nor had she assured him she wouldn't get any worse. Hell, he had no idea what was going on in that head of hers. And Felix wasn't about to go down the road of brain disorders again. It might be coldhearted of him, but he simply could not risk caring about someone only to lose them the way he had Megan. He was not going to do it. *Nunca más*. Never again.

He focused on mixing the flowers into his meal instead of on Rory. And he told her, "Let me get back to you. We're booked solid through the end of the comet festival."

Which wasn't entirely true. They had a handful of tables open for the upcoming week. And he always made room for his friends. But what tables he had wouldn't last long. With this kind of action in town, no way was Felix ever going to have a night without a full house. As for the *always mak-*

ing room for his friends… Well. He wasn't sure he and Rory had reached that point yet.

He could tell she was disappointed by his reply. He forced himself to focus on his meal instead of on her, but all he could do was push his food from one side of the box to the other.

After a few awkward moments, Rory said, "This is delicious. I've never had Cuban food before."

Felix finally did look up at that. "Are you sure?"

The smile she had clearly been forcing fell. "No. I'm not. See? I said something dumb. Again."

He shook his head. "I'm sorry. I shouldn't have asked that. You're not being dumb. I'm being insensitive. I'm just not sure what I'm supposed to say to someone who has…"

He still couldn't say the word out loud. It was just so weird.

"Which is exactly why I haven't told anyone about my condition," she said. "The only reason I told you was because you're the first person who's said or done something that made me actually remember something. As difficult as it is for you to hear me talk about it, how do you think I feel to be living it?"

At that, he relented. Some. "Look. Rory. I'm not the key to your past. I can't be the key to your past."

She sighed heavily. "I know that, Felix. I do. But you're the closest thing I've got so far. No one else has done or said anything that's shaken free a memory."

Felix was about to speak again, but she took a taste of her soda and nearly choked on it. Her hand flew to her mouth to keep her from spitting it out, then she struggled to swallow.

"Oh my god!" she fairly shouted when she could finally speak again. "I've had this before! I've tasted Coco Rico!"

"But you said you didn't recognize it," Felix protested.

"I didn't. But I do now. I mean, the can didn't look familiar, but I've absolutely had this to drink before. I love this. It's one of my favorite things to drink."

Felix shook his head. Nobody drank Coco Rico unless they had some kind of tie to the Caribbean. Or at least to Latino communities. How could it be one of her favorite drinks?

She closed her eyes and took another sip, taking her time to enjoy it. Then her eyes flew open. "I remember sitting at a table drinking this," she said. "In a kitchen somewhere. With my lunch. There was a woman cooking at the stove, and a girl—a girl I know I knew, but I can't remember her face or her name—sitting across from me. There was a vase of flowers on the table, too," she added, her excitement doubling. "Hibiscus and butterfly pea. They were beautiful. And there were guavas and avocados on the countertop. Felix, the image is so clear! It's like I'm sitting right there!"

In spite of his aversion to her condition, Felix's heart began to pound. "Do you know who the woman is? Who the girl is? I mean, not so much their names, but what kind of relationship you shared with them?"

She closed her eyes again, as if she were trying very hard to recall. But when she opened them again, he was amazed to see they were filled with tears. She really was trying hard to remember. And she really was heartbroken that she couldn't.

She shook her head and reached for the paper napkin by her box. Dabbing at her eyes, she told him, "No. But they were important to me somehow. I just don't know how." She sniffled, then touched the napkin to her eyes again. "I remember that I loved them, Felix. But I can't remember who they are."

Strangely, his disappointment was nearly as profound as hers. He told himself to get a grip.

"See?" she said with a final wipe of her eyes. She looked at him as if he were the answer to every prayer she'd sent skyward. "You're my link,

Felix. There's something about you, something about your experiences that have a common link with my own. Even your cat—"

"My grandmother's cat," he said, correcting her again. Although, after the way Nestor had responded to Rory a little while ago, maybe he should gift the animal to her.

"Even your grandmother's cat," she amended, "brought back a memory I hadn't had until today. The only way I'm going to figure out who I am and where I come from is through you. Please, I am begging you, just let me hang around with you. Let me talk to you. Let me see the world through your eyes. Because there's something there that's going to help me. I just know it."

It was a bad idea. Felix knew it deep down in a part of himself that was always quick to say, *I told you so*. It was an inner voice he'd heard all his life, one he knew he should listen to. But just as he always had before, he dismissed it.

"All right," he told her. "We can spend some time together. But don't get your hopes up."

And he wouldn't get his up, either. 'Cause that, he knew, would be the biggest mistake of all.

Rory and Felix finished their lunch in relatively genial conversation about everything except each other, and when they'd cleaned up the remnants, they turned to the task of all the clutter and scattered belongings and half-filled boxes. It still looked to Rory like he was packing to move out. But she learned quickly that it was more like he was packing to move on.

"Where can I help?" she asked.

Felix sighed as he considered the mess. "You know, this seemed like a good idea last night, but now..."

"And what exactly does this previously good idea involve?"

He continued to look at the state of the apartment instead of at her. "This apartment hasn't changed at all since I was a little kid," he said. "I mean, except for the addition of some things to commemorate life's little celebrations, this place is exactly the way Tita furnished it when she moved in. I've never seen it look any different."

As he spoke, Rory couldn't help realizing that where she had no memories of her own past, Felix must have a flood of them from his own.

"It was fine when my grandmother was alive," he said. "This was her place. And, frankly, except for my bedroom, I barely paid attention to it while I was growing up." He chuckled, but there wasn't a lot of happiness in the sound. "Hell, even my bedroom has hardly changed since I was a teenager. I still have a bunch of Star Wars LEGOs and Hot Wheels on my book case."

Living in a teenager's bedroom was so unlike her image of the super-successful, always-in-charge Felix Suarez that Rory had to physically stop herself from darting down the hall to check on the veracity of his statement.

Oh, who was she kidding?

"This, I gotta see," she told him as she headed in that direction.

Surprisingly, he did nothing to stop her. Instead, he followed her. His room was the first one she encountered, and she immediately saw that he hadn't been lying. Not only was there still a single bed in there—and Rory honestly wasn't sure what to make of that, other than that he must never bring women home, which could be significant for a lot of reasons she'd mull later—but there were indeed more LEGOs and Hot Wheels than she could shake a stick at. There were also some action figures of indeterminate origin and collections of natural debris, such as rocks and sticks and other things kids picked up and didn't want to let go of for whatever reason. There were posters, too, one for a blue creature identified as Sonic the Hedgehog and another of a soccer player in a blue-and-red jersey. But there was a noticeably bare spot on one wall.

"What was there?" Rory asked. "Looks like something's not quite the way it used to be."

"Okay, I lied," he admitted. "I did change one thing. I took down my Avril Lavigne poster when I was fourteen, after she got married. I could never forgive her for not waiting for me."

Rory smiled, but Felix was still assessing his room as if seeing it for the first time.

"I really haven't paid any attention to this space for a while, have I?" he muttered.

"Oh, I don't know," she told him. "I think it's kind of charming. In a retro, wow-this-guy-is-still-sleeping-in-a-single-bed kind of way."

He gave her an only slightly teasing side-eye. "I don't really, um, entertain much at home."

Once again, Rory decided that was something she could think about later. Which was good, since Felix kept going with his decor assessment.

"I should probably at least replace my Lionel Messi poster with one for Louisville FC." Now he gave her a look that made her think he was carefully weighing what he wanted to say next. "Max and I have season tickets. I could probably talk him out of his for one night. Maybe you and I could take in a match sometime."

She was too surprised to reply. He'd actually sounded kind of spirited when he made the offer.

But when she didn't respond right away, he

waved his hand dismissively. "I mean, just to see if maybe soccer does anything to jog your memory. Like, maybe if you ever went to a match, you might remember where it was, and that could possibly tell you something about where you lived. You know?"

"I'd love to go to a match," she told him. "Thanks."

And she realized when she said it that it wasn't solely because it might jog her memory. She was feeling kind of spirited about the prospect, too.

Before her spiritedness could turn into something else, she told him, "You're right. You seriously need to update your space. Have you ever thought about turning this room into an office or something, and moving yourself into your grandmother's bedroom? I'm sure it's bigger than this one."

Part of her thought he might disregard the suggestion outright. And, really, it wasn't her place to propose it. Instead, he looked over his shoulder, through his bedroom door, toward the room in question. "It is bigger," he said. "And it has its own bathroom. Tita actually tried to trade rooms with me after I graduated from high school. She said since I'd gotten to be twice as tall as her, I should have the bigger room. But it felt too weird to do it then. She was still the head of the household. Still made the rules. But now..."

He looked at Rory again.

"Now?" she asked.

He shrugged. "I don't know. She's been gone two years, but it still seems like it would be weird to move into her space. Especially since—" He halted abruptly before finishing.

"Especially since what?" she asked.

"Especially since I'm not planning to stay in Endicott that much longer."

The admission surprised her. A lot. "But why? La Mariposa is doing so well. And this is your home."

"La Mariposa is doing well," he agreed. "So well, in fact, that I'm looking into opening a couple more in bigger markets."

"Like Louisville?" she asked.

He shook his head. "It's a great city for restaurants, but I'm looking to go even bigger than that."

"Indianapolis?" she said, surprised to hear a hopefulness in her voice she hadn't been aware of feeling. "Cincinnati? Nashville?"

They were all good-sized cities within a two- or three-hour drive of Endicott. Even Chicago was close enough to drive in half a day. She started to ask if that last one was a possibility, too, but something stopped her. There was something about the thought of Chicago that made her feel uneasy. It was the same feeling she'd had when she and Min had driven around the city shortly after Rory's release from the hospital, to see if maybe any of the sights spurred her memory. None had. But the city itself had felt oppressive and menacing. After only thirty minutes of looking around, Rory had wanted desperately to escape. Not leave. Not go back to Gary. But *escape*. That was how she had felt.

Which had ultimately been kind of helpful, in spite of making her feel so intimidated by the place. When she was still in the hospital, Min had splashed Rory's image all over Chicago media, thinking maybe she was from there. But no one had come forward to ID her. No one in Indianapolis, another city Min had focused on, had identified Rory, either, but the thought of that city didn't rouse any kind of feelings in her at all. Certainly not the way the thought of Chicago did. Nausea rolled through her belly again as she thought about it, and she had to fight back a feeling of dread. She was sure there was a reason for her feeling the way she did about the Windy City. But damned if she knew what it was.

"Maybe Indianapolis for my first effort," Felix said, pulling her back to the present. Thank goodness. "But ultimately, I want to go even bigger. Miami, probably, next. Then, hopefully, New York."

"Wow," Rory said. "Those would both be a huge change from Endicott."

"Yeah, but I have some friends and extended family in Miami, at least, and I've visited a lot. Tita and I used to go down there every summer for vacation. It would be competitive. There are a lot of Cuban restaurants there. But there's also a much bigger market for Cuban and Caribbean food."

"But, even with friends there, it's so far from your roots here," she said.

She wasn't sure why she was trying to dissuade him. It was his life. His dream. But Felix was fast becoming her biggest tie to Endicott. In spite of the fact that she was just now getting to know him, she was having trouble imagining living here with him off somewhere else.

"Do you have friends in New York, too?" she asked.

He shook his head. "Nada. But I want a Michelin star. Or two. Or three. And they only award those in the US in a handful of cities. New York has more Michelin-starred restaurants than any other city in this country."

There went her stomach again.

"I could do a lot in New York," he continued. He sighed with much satisfaction. "Yeah, that would be the place to make it."

It was strange that Rory was so surprised by his desire to move away from Endicott and his roots. She had no idea where her own roots were, or even how deep they might be wherever that was. She'd only been in his hometown for a couple of months, but she already couldn't imagine living anywhere else. It just felt so cozy here. So down-to-earth. So safe. So right.

"So what will happen to La Mariposa here?" she asked. "I mean, surely, you won't close it, right? It's so popular."

"I would never close this place," he assured her. "Tita would haunt me forever if I did. But Tinima will be a great executive chef. Hell, she could run the place right now, if I stepped down."

Wow, he really was ready to move on, Rory thought. She was surprised how much that bothered her.

"Well, if you're eventually going to be moving," she said, "then you're right. This place needs updating before you can rent it out to someone else."

"Nah, I'll keep the restaurant but sell the apartment. No reason to hang on to it."

Not unless maybe he wanted to come back to Endicott someday. Which, clearly, he didn't intend to do.

"Oh. Well. Okay," Rory replied. "All the more

reason to spiff it up as best you can. I can help you," she added hopefully.

"You know about home decorating, too?"

"I don't think so. But I know what colors look good with other colors. And how much harder can it be to arrange furniture than it is flowers? Once you figure out the color scheme, it all comes down to balance and orientation."

"If you say so."

"Seriously, Felix, I can help. If you'll let me."

She hoped he didn't hear the odd twist of longing in her voice that she detected—and wondered about—herself. Surely all the strange feelings that had been coursing through her since arriving at Felix's place today were the result of a desire to fit in and belong somewhere, which was how she was beginning to feel about Endicott. Surely, there was nothing more to it than that. Surely.

But Felix seemed not to notice her disquiet, because he only strode to his bedroom door and exited, passing a bathroom to stop at the entrance to the second bedroom. Rory followed, arriving just as he turned on the overhead light.

It was the quintessential grandma room, from the sturdy mahogany furniture, to the handmade floral quilt on the bed, to the watercolor prints of Caribbean coastlines, to the—

"Oh my god," Rory said with a chuckle as she moved to the far corner of the room.

—to the photos of Felix from the time he was a baby, up to what looked like just a few years ago.

"Oh my god, Felix, these are adorable."

"Yeah, yeah, yeah," he said with resolve as he came to stand beside her.

"You were awfully cute when you were little," she told him, pointing to a faded image of a laughing, chubby little baby.

"Yeah, I never missed a meal, that's for sure."

"And is this the first day of school?" she asked, indicating another. "Love the bow tie. Not many six-year-olds could pull that off, you know."

"I was a trendsetter."

She noted another one of Felix and two little boys she was pretty sure grew up to be the two friends she saw him with most often. Chance and Max, were their names, she recalled now. "This can't possibly be you with Chance and Max."

"Yeah, it is," he said. "That was at Camp Palawopec, in Brown County, when we were eight."

"You guys have been friends for a long time."

"Practically since birth. Best times of my life were with those guys."

It struck her again how easily he spoke of moving elsewhere. He had friends here he'd loved for decades. She doubted that even if she did regain her memory, she would be able to cop to that. Not many people could. How was he going to leave behind so much that was so familiar and go someplace entirely new to start his life all over? Didn't he realize how valuable memories and history were? If she had either, there was nothing she would treasure more.

"I don't know, Felix. I think it's going to be harder to leave Endicott than you think."

"You just say that because you've only been here a couple of months. Try growing up someplace like this. Nothing ever happens here. I've been dying to get out of here since I was a teenager. It was boring as hell when I was a kid."

Rory looked at the array of photos on the wall again, pictures of Felix on boats and skateboards, hugging a giant dog and feeding a baby pig, hewing a tree and planting flowers, wearing a soccer uniform, prom tux, graduation gown, chef's whites… Didn't look like a boring life to her at all. She only hoped she had a fraction of his memories when she finally regained her own.

"The restaurant is closed tomorrow," she heard him say behind her. "Think you could steal away from work for a few hours and help me figure out how to whip this place into shape?"

Tomorrow was Monday. Her slowest day of the week. She could spare more than a few hours.

"Ezra opens tomorrow, and I have another full-timer coming in. Becca has been saying she wants some extra hours. If she can make it, I can take the whole day tomorrow."

"Great," he said brightly. "We can finish up what I started out in the living room today, then start in here tomorrow." He shook his head at the collection of photographs on his grandmother's wall. "First thing to go is The Great Wall of Felix."

Oh, those pictures weren't *going* anywhere, Rory decided on the spot. She'd box up Felix's memories herself and stow them someplace in her own apartment where they would stay safe. Someday, he'd be glad he had them. Because someday, when he was living far from home, far from his friends, far from his memories and history, he'd realize just how lonely a life with none of those things was. And he'd realize just how much all of them were worth.

More than all the Michelin stars in the world.

Chapter Six

Felix was one of those people who never, ever, owned up to making a mistake. Number one, he made so few of them, it was almost never necessary. And two, he didn't like to think of the few mistakes he had made as *mistakes*. They were actually *episodes*. Episodes that had provided a learning opportunity of something new or an example of what to avoid in the future.

Today, however, for the first time in his life, he was willing to concede that maybe, possibly, perhaps, he had made a mistake in allowing Rory to help him declutter his apartment. It wasn't just because she looked way too damned adorable in cut-off shorts and a T-shirt decorated with a giant sunflower—even though *adorable* was one of those words he normally, manfully, avoided, which was why he had prefaced it with profanity. Even worse than the damned adorableness, though, was that the two of them were uncovering way too many things from his past that he really would have rather left buried.

He especially never should have allowed her into his grandmother's room. He couldn't believe how many trappings of his childhood and adolescence Tita had saved over the years. Things like the tiny wooden spoon he'd discovered in his Christmas stocking when he was three because the ones in the kitchen, where he was spending more and more of his time at that point, were too big for his little toddler hands. And the blue ribbon he won at the Indiana State Fair when he was twelve, for his Cuban sugar cookies—the dark rum and dulce de leche had been his secret weapons. Tita had even kept the cardboard and velveteen crown he'd won as Endicott High School's homecoming king his junior year.

Talk about embarrassing. And when he'd refused to put it on, Rory had called him a party pooper and decided to wear it herself. She was still wearing it. Which made her even more damned adorable.

Dammit.

"Oh my god!" she cried now over one of the many boxes they'd pulled from his grandmother's closet. "A sock puppet wearing a little chef's hat! Did you make this?"

She withdrew a crumpled rag sock with a badly stitched mouth and only one googly eye left, not to mention the aforementioned toque. Which looked more like a toilet paper tube painted white—which it was—so props to her for figuring it out. Felix squeezed his eyes shut. Of course he'd made it. Who the hell else would have made a monstrosity like that?

He sighed. He might as well come clean. No way was she going to let it go. She hadn't let anything go all day. Not only had he had to tell her all about his state fair and homecoming experiences, but she now also knew about him failing his driver's test the first time, how a book titled *Babosa Va al Baño* taught him to use the potty, and how he'd been laid up one summer with the worst case of poison ivy in the history of sleep-away camps named with obscure—and, these days, culturally inappropriate—Indian names. These were things he would just as soon not be made public to the women in his life.

Not that Rory was a woman in his life. Not that

Rory would ever *be* a woman in his life. It was the principle of the thing.

Very reluctantly, he admitted, "Yeah. I made it. That's *El Jefe de Cocina* Javier. Head Chef Javier," he translated for her. Since it had become clear over the past couple of days that, however she knew Spanish, it wasn't kitchen-related. "It was a school assignment when I was in first grade. We had to make a puppet of what we wanted to be when we grew up."

"And there are two others," she said, pulling the other socks out of the box behind Javier.

He shrugged. "I had fun with it, so I ended up making a whole kitchen of puppets. The other ones you have there are Javier's expo…his expediter," he quickly clarified when she looked up, confused. "His name is Banjo. No, I don't know why I named him Banjo," he replied before Rory could ask, since she was obviously about to ask. "I was only six. And the other one is a maître d'."

But he didn't mention that one's name, because… Because he didn't want to. That was why.

"What's his name?" Rory asked anyway.

He expelled a restless sound. "*Her* name," he said. "My maître d' was a girl." But he still didn't mention her name.

"How very progressive of you," she said. And then, inescapably, she added, "What's her name?"

Felix stumbled a little as he replied, "Meg… Um… Megan. Her name was…is… Megan."

After the best friend he'd had in art class. The one who, even then, had already undertaken her battle with a disease that would eventually take her life. Not that Felix—or any of the other kids—had known that at the time. And not that he was going to tell Rory about any of that now.

Not that Rory was going to let it go.

"Interesting choice for a maître d' name," she said. "I mean, considering the other two are Javier and Banjo, which are both kind of exotic."

"Yeah, kids are stupid," he said as he snatched the three puppets from her hands and tossed them into the box holding all the other stuff he'd be hauling down to the dumpster tonight.

"Wait, aren't you going to keep those?" she asked.

"Why would I keep those?"

She seemed stumped for a moment. "I don't know. Because you made them? Because they're a part of your past?"

"I've made lots of things in my life, Rory. If I kept every one of them, I'd be on the next episode of *Hoarders*."

He couldn't believe how crestfallen she looked, knowing he was going to throw out some old socks that had stuff glued on them—badly at that—just because they were a part of his past. Even Nestor was glaring at him with much accusation from his place at the foot of Tita's bed.

Then Felix reminded himself that Rory couldn't remember her own past. Even so, he bet if there were homemade sock puppets in it somewhere, she'd probably gotten rid of them a long time ago. She only thought it was important to hold on to stuff like Javier and Banjo and— She only thought it was important to hold on to stuff like that because she didn't have any physical reminders of her own past.

She looked like she wanted to argue with him, but she didn't. Instead, she went back to the box she was going through, one they'd pulled down from the very top shelf in his grandmother's closet. The farther up they'd gone with Tita's keepsakes, the older and more obscure they'd gotten. At this rate, it wouldn't be long before they turned up his first pair of big-boy underwear. The ones with the little hot dogs and hamburgers on them.

Dios mío*, Tita. Did you have to keep everything I ever touched?*

He looked at Rory again. Great. She'd just found another stack of photos. There better not be any with him as a naked baby. To this day, whenever Tori Leiberman ran into him in town, she still needled him about the bearskin rug picture Tita showed her on prom night.

But Rory found one far, far worse than that.

"Is this your mom?" she asked as she turned a photo toward him. It was a rhetorical question, he knew. There was no way the woman in the photo could *not* be Felix's mother. She looked just like him.

Felix went stiff when he saw it. It was the only picture his grandmother had kept of her only child, framed but never displayed. For a moment, he avoided looking at it. He'd seen it before, of course, but a few times had been more than enough. Even so, it had probably been a couple of decades since the last time, so he gave it a quick glance before going back to the box he'd been sorting through himself.

"Yep," he told her dispassionately.

She waited to see if he would add anything to the single-syllable response. He didn't.

"You look just like her," Rory said.

"I look just like my grandmother," he amended.

She'd seen enough photos of him and his grandmother by now to be familiar with Tita's image. "She and your mom look a lot alike, too," she said. "You look more like your mother than your grandmother, though."

"I beg to differ."

She said nothing for a moment, then looked at the photo again. "Strong genes on the female side of your family."

"Strong females on the female side of my family," he said, correcting her again. He, too, hesitated a moment before adding, "Except for one." His mother had taken off at the first sign of adversity in her life. The prospect of motherhood.

Rory opened her mouth to say something—obviously, she knew who he was talking about—then seemed to think better of it. Instead, she studied the photo again, this time with more scrutiny.

"The cross you wear," she said. "That belonged to your mom."

He continued to toss items from his box into one headed for the dumpster. "No, it belonged to my grandmother," he said without looking up.

Rory pushed the photo under his nose so that he couldn't avoid seeing it. "Sure looks like the one in this picture to me."

Knowing she wasn't going to leave it alone, he took the photo from her, considering it as if for the first time. In a way, he was. He'd never given it more than a passing glance. He'd never wanted to *consider* it. He lifted a finger to first trace the necklace in the photo, then touch it to the gold crucifix draped around his neck. Rory was right. It was the same one.

"Tita gave this to me when I made my First Communion. She said it had been in her family for six generations. I just assumed it was coming straight from her."

"Your mom must have left it behind for you. She obviously wanted you to have it. Maybe because, on some level, she thought she wasn't able to give you anything else."

Felix said nothing, only looked at the photo one last time and returned to his task. Rory stood and carried the photo of his mother across the room to place it carefully in the box of pictures of him that she'd taken off the wall earlier. The ones she thought he was going to save, and he hadn't dissuaded her from that assumption. No way was he going to tell her those were going to the dumpster tonight, too. Now so more than ever.

In a soft voice, she said, "They told me at the hospital that I'd never given birth, but that doesn't mean I might not have a stepchild or adopted child out there somewhere. There's a chance, even if it's a small one, that some kid out there thinks their mother abandoned them, when in fact she's running a flower shop in Endicott, Indiana, because she doesn't know who she is."

He expelled a sound of disbelief at that. "Oh,

what, now you're going to try to tell me my mother took off because *she* has no memories of her past?"

She looked at him and sighed heavily. "No, Felix. I'm saying that if your grandmother never told you the necklace belonged to your mother, then there are probably other things she never told you about your mother. Like maybe why she left in the first place."

"No. She didn't," he admitted, still not looking up from his task. "But I never asked, either. What difference does it make? She wanted something else. Something better. I can't fault her for that. It's the same thing I want. She probably hated this place, too."

Now Rory made her way back to sit on the floor next to Felix, closer than she'd been before. She was still within reach of the box she'd been sorting through, but she didn't go back to that. Instead, she looked at Felix.

"Number one," she said, "I don't think you hate this place. I think you love it." Before he had a chance to object, she continued, "And number two, my point is that you don't know why your mother took off. Maybe you should give her the benefit of the doubt."

"Yeah, okay, fine."

"Felix..." Whatever she'd intended to say, she

didn't finish. Maybe she didn't know what she wanted to say.

Which made two of them. In spite of that, Felix told her, "Look, Rory. I don't even remember my mother. I only remember Tita. And she was solid as a rock. She made sure every day that I knew how much she loved me. She made sure my life was stable. Yeah, I'm sure there's unresolved… stuff…inside me about my mother taking off. But it's not what defines my life, okay? Like I told you before, it's what we are now that matters."

She nodded with resignation. Felix didn't belabor the point. He understood how frustrating it must be for her to not know the reasons for why she was the person she was. But she also seemed to realize it was pointless to continue the conversation, and for that, he was grateful. She was about to reach for her box again when something in his caught her eye instead. She dipped her hand into it, pushing aside yet another homemade birthday card he'd given his grandmother at some point to pull out a photo of a girl he remembered from a few trips he and Tita had taken to Miami when he was a kid.

"Who's this?" she asked.

"That's Tita's goddaughter, Alicia," Felix told her. "I didn't know her that well. She was a few years older than me."

"She looks like a Disney princess."

She wasn't wrong. In the photo, Alicia was wearing a rhinestone tiara and a bright emerald ball gown spattered with sequins. Her hair was a riot of curls, and her makeup was a little heavier than a teenage girl would normally wear.

"Yeah, that was taken at her *quinceañera,*" he said.

Rory snapped her head up at that, looking at him with wide eyes and her mouth agape.

He thought she was confused, so he explained, "It's sort of like a Sweet Sixteen party in a lot of Hispanic communities, only it happens when girls turn fifteen. The dress is always a major thing."

She looked back at the photo, but seemed to be lost in thought. She started digging deeper into the box, until she found a few more photos from the same event and studied them one by one. One in particular captured her fancy. It was of Alicia surrounded by girls of a similar age, also dressed up, but not quite like, as Rory had said, Disney princesses. Their dresses, though, were identical to each other and complemented the party girl's. It wasn't a whole lot different from pictures of brides with their bridesmaids.

Rory pointed at the photo and smiled. "I've been to one of these," she said.

"You've been to a quinceañera," Felix said dubiously.

She nodded. "I have. I know I have. I can smell the flowers and cigar smoke. I can taste the *tres leches* cake. I remember dancing to a song that went..."

She started humming, slowly at first, then picking up speed as the memory must have become clearer. She even started swaying the upper part of her body and went into some halfway decent beatboxing as if she were DJ RoryRoar or something. Finally, she was doing so well with it that, even without the lyrics, Felix knew exactly what song she was performing. And when she got to the chorus—

"Da me mas gas-o-lina," he sang as if he were one of the miniskirted backup singers in the music video he'd watched a million times when he was a teenager. Cars, beautiful girls and rebellion. What wasn't to love?

"Yes!" she cried. "That was it! That's the song I remember!"

The two of them sang the chorus together for a moment—well, Felix sang, and Rory sort of elided along—then he continued on his own, singing the next verse as she accompanied him with her vocal percussions, her body swaying even more, until she was bumping into him in time to the music. Then they sang the refrain together one last time, laughing when it was finally over.

Felix had no idea why he felt so good in that moment. Maybe because it was a relief to not be talking about his mother. Maybe because their impromptu concert had alleviated some of the stress that had knotted him since he started going through his grandmother's things. Maybe just because, in that moment, there was just something very fun going on. He didn't know what, but he liked that whatever it was, it was happening with Rory. He told himself it was just because he hadn't heard that song in a long time and had once loved it, and she had just given him one of those rare gifts of a happy memory that came out of nowhere to make him feel good. But there was more to it than that. He just wasn't sure what.

Then she was looking at him, and he was looking at her, and their laughter suddenly started to ebb. The room shrank around him, until there didn't seem to be anything in the world but him and Rory. She was still wearing his ridiculous prom king crown, still looking damned adorable. She smelled good, too, he couldn't help noticing, something clean and herby that was mixing in with the aroma of his grandmother's *Flor y Canto* perfume that somehow still lingered among her possessions.

It was an intriguing blend of fragrances, of both the past and the present, just as the vision of Rory sitting there in his prom crown was. For a moment, Felix honestly wasn't sure where he was—when he was—and before he realized what he was doing, he was dipping his head toward hers. It wasn't until Rory tipped her own head backward and closed her eyes that he realized what he was doing. Then he snapped his whole body backward, shoving his hand back into the box he'd been working on, focusing on its contents as hard as he could.

But his heart was hammering, his head was spinning, and he couldn't quite get a grip on his thoughts. Or his feelings. Or much of anything else. All he could think about was how much he wanted to kiss Rory. And touch Rory. And make love to Rory. And holy hell, there was no way he could do any of those things. Not when everything in her life was a giant question mark. Not when everything in his life was starting to feel that way, too.

"*Any*way," he said, forcing a steadiness into his voice he was nowhere close to feeling, "the song is called 'Gasolina,' and it was recorded by Daddy Yankee, and the genre of music is called reggaeton, and that song was very popular in the Latin community when it came out, and—"

And *dios mío*, could he just stop talking? He wanted to look at Rory, but didn't dare. He didn't even know what to say at that point. Not until he realized something really interesting.

"That song probably came out about the time you were fifteen," he said, still staring into his box. Not that he thought Rory had been the one celebrating the quinceañera she remembered. But… "And seeing as you were at a quinceañera at the time, your friend was fifteen, too."

For a long moment, she didn't say anything. Felix kept his attention trained utterly and completely on the box beside him, even though he barely saw or felt anything that was in it, because he was too busy reliving the vision of Rory closing her eyes in anticipation of the kiss he very nearly gave her. Finally, she scooted back over to where she'd been sitting before, a couple of feet away from him. Only then was Felix able to expel a breath he hadn't even been aware of holding. Only then could he halfway think clearly again.

"If you were fifteen the same time as your friend," Felix said, "and according to when that song came out, it would make you twenty-eight years old now."

Rory said nothing in response to that. When

Felix finally braved a glance at her, it was to find that she was as fake-fascinated with the box in front of her as he'd been with his. She didn't rejoice in the knowledge of her age, even though it was clear the revelation had staggered her.

She looked up at Felix with a half smile. "I remember something else from that day. I was wearing this pink frilly dress made out of some super-scratchy material that had lace and glitter all over it. And high heels," she added, sounding even more mystified. "I mean, they weren't real high heels, but they *were* heels. It was the first time I'd ever worn heels. Somehow, I'm positive of that. And I was having trouble walking around in them. I had to take them off to dance. And I remember thinking I would never in my life wear a pink frilly dress with all that froufy crap on it, or high heels I could barely walk in. That the only person in the entire world I would put on a pink frilly dress and high heels for would be..."

Here, she stopped, closing her eyes again, tighter than before, as if she were thinking very hard. For one long moment, she was silent as she concentrated. Then she expelled an irritated sound and opened her eyes again.

"I don't remember," she finally finished. "Not a date. Not a boy. I'm sure of that. A best friend. But I don't remember her name or what she looked like or where we lived. I just know she was my best friend, and that…" Here, she finally looked at him. "And that I went to her quinceañera. I know I did, Felix. I know it."

Every time she regained some kind of memory, Felix grew more confused. He was reasonably certain she wasn't Latina. But she sure did seem to have a lot of memories of Hispanic culture. She'd been walking around Endicott, a thoroughly Midwestern, completely average, as-American-as-apple-pie town for months without recognizing a single thing about herself or her past. But a few days with his Latino self, and she'd started having regular flashes of memory more suited to him than to her.

"Daddy Yankee is Puerto Rican," he said, thinking it might help trigger another memory. "Any chance your friend was Puerto Rican, too? Or that you maybe lived in Puerto Rico?"

She let it sink in, then shook her head. "I don't think I lived in Puerto Rico," she said. "But maybe my friend was Puerto Rican." She growled under her breath. "This is so frustrating. It's like there are memories at the very edges of my brain, taunting me but not coming forward."

Felix couldn't imagine what that must be like. He had so many memories, of so many things, he wasn't sure he could even catalogue them in his brain if he tried. And he just took for granted that they'd always be there, either for him to conjure up willingly when he needed them, or to pop up and surprise him when someone mentioned something he thought he'd forgotten about.

Rory couldn't enjoy either of those experiences right now. He'd started to wonder if maybe her life prior to her amnesia had just been so full of bad things that, on some level, her brain had decided to block it all out. But if she was remembering things like drinking Coco Rico in someone's kitchen full of flowers and going to a quinceañera, then she'd at least had some good times in her past.

And they were good times she couldn't remember. He'd hate it if he lost his memories of Tita or Chance and Max. Or even Megan, as hard as it was to remember her—and he'd been remembering her a lot over the past couple of days. All of them had been a huge part of the best times of Felix's life. For his brain to be full of darkness and confusion instead would be awful.

He'd been thinking all day that this would be the last day the two of them would spend together. That he was going to have to put Rory at arm's length and keep her there, if for no other reason than to preserve his own sanity. But if he was the only link she had to recovering even a handful of memories of a life that had at least been happy on occasion—and it was pretty clear that he was the only link for that—then he'd be a complete bastard not to help her out. He just wished he knew what to do to help. The sooner, the better.

"How about some lunch?" he asked.

She nodded wearily. "Thanks. I am getting hungry."

Felix was, too. But more than that, he needed a break. A break from the past, where he'd spent way too much time today. He wasn't one to live in the past. He was much more interested in the future. A future that wouldn't include anything here in Endicott, save for La Mariposa. And even his restaurant was now more a kind of springboard to launch him into the next phase of his life away from here.

Yeah, the future. That was where it was at. Now, more than ever, Felix wanted to start making serious plans for it.

Chapter Seven

Monday night found Felix joining his friends Chance and Max in Chance's backyard, where they sat around a fire in the firepit as the embers in the nearby grill slowly turned to ash. Chance had grilled for them all tonight so that Felix and Max could meet his newly acquired family—a niece and nephew, twins—who were now his wards following the death of his estranged brother. At the moment, the kids were running around the back of the yard with their new puppy and their temporary guardian, Poppy, chasing fireflies and ignoring her admonitions to put their shoes back on. As had been the case for a good part of the evening, Chance's gaze currently seemed to be more on Poppy than on the kids, something Felix had mixed feelings about. On one hand, it was good to see his friend interested in a woman who had the potential to be more than a lightweight fling, as most of Chance's girlfriends turned out to be. On the other hand, Poppy was only in town long enough to get the children settled before she had to return to her job back in Boston. There wasn't going to be much of an opportunity for anything to get started in Endicott. Or, if something did start, to finish here.

"So let me get this straight," Max said beside him. "Your next-door neighbor can't remember *any*thing prior to New Year's Eve?"

Felix hadn't planned to tell his friends about Rory's amnesia, since it seemed like one of those personal things about a friend he should just keep to himself—even if Rory was starting to feel like more than a friend. But as happened so often when the three men got together, one thing led to another, and somebody—tonight it was him—ended up saying more than they intended. Like the time in middle school when Chance admitted he had a thing for Iris Fernsby, Endicott's resident goth girl and Disneyphile. Or that night in high school when *Miss Congeniality* came on while they were channel surfing during a sleepover, and Max copped to actually kind of enjoying romantic comedies.

"Nothing substantial," Felix replied. "She's having flashes of memory here and there about things from when she was a kid, but nothing more recent. And nothing that really tells her who she is or where she's from."

"So she could be anybody," Chance said.

"From anywhere," Max added. "Holy crow."

"Yeah," Felix agreed, his stomach still churning a bit at the realization.

"That's crazy," Max said.

For some reason, Felix's hackles went up at that. "She's not crazy," he said coolly.

So coolly, evidently, that Max and Chance both looked at him with concern.

"I didn't say Rory is crazy," Max pointed out. "I said the situation is crazy."

"Sorry," Felix said. "It's just..." Now he relaxed some and sighed. "It's just...weird. Rory's a nice person, a good person, and she shouldn't have—"

"Nice?" Chance echoed before Felix could finish. "Good? You've never called her nice or good before. That's what you call Arjun's pastries."

"Yeah," Max agreed. "You've called Rory 'smoking hot' and 'icy cool'..."

"And 'spicy deliciousness' and 'damned tasty,'" Chance added.

"And 'dazzling,'" Max said with a smile. "Don't forget when he called her 'dazzling.'"

Chance laughed lightly. "And 'supah fine.' Remember 'supah fine'?"

"Oh, yeah," Max replied, chuckling. "And he hadn't even been drinking."

The two men laughed some more. Felix glared. "Are you done?" he asked his friends.

They shared another moment of hilarity, then eased off. Mostly. They were both still looking at him as if they were all back in school again, and he'd just admitted to liking Iris Fernsby and romantic comedies.

"*Any*way," Felix continued, "as I was saying. Rory is a *nice*, *good* person. She shouldn't have to be going through something like this."

Max sobered. "And you want to help her."

Felix met his friend's gaze. "Yeah. I do."

Normally, that would have been a strange thing for him to say. *Helpful* wasn't a word many people ascribed to Felix. In fact, he doubted anyone had ever called him helpful. He knew that. And, honestly, before now, it never bothered him. It wasn't that he didn't want to help people out. It was just that it never occurred to him to do it. He didn't like to think he was self-absorbed. But maybe, in a way, he kind of was. Especially since his grandmother's death, he'd been so focused on what the future held for him that he hadn't really given much thought about what anyone else was doing or planning to do. He'd only known he wanted to move on with his life, as soon as possible, somewhere other than here. Because he just hadn't felt like there was anything here for him anymore.

Now he looked at his friends. What were Max and Chance going to say when he told them he was leaving Endicott for someplace like Miami or New York? Or even Indianapolis? Yeah, it was only a couple hours away, but if he moved up there, would there really be many opportunities to come back here? Would there really be many reasons? All three of them were pretty involved with their own jobs and lives. And Chance had two kids to take care of now. It was starting to look like maybe the future had plans for all three of them that didn't include the others.

The idea didn't sit well with Felix. For the first time, he gave some serious thought about what his life would be like if—no, when—he left his hometown behind, beyond just opening a new restaurant. He'd be completely alone somewhere else. He'd have to build all new relationships, not just professional, but personal, too. He'd have to figure out how to maneuver his new physical surroundings and learn which places to frequent and which to avoid. There wouldn't be any more nights sitting around a grill with his friends razzing him good-naturedly and him razzing them in return. No more saying hello to his colleagues in Old Town Endicott every time he walked down Water Street. Hell, he'd be in an urban environment where people on the street barely acknowledged each other.

But that was good, right? It meant he'd be filling his life and his head with new things to excite him that would chase out the old things he didn't want to dwell on. Tita. Megan.

Rory.

"So what are you going to do?" Chance asked him.

It took a moment for Felix to realize his friend wasn't talking about his plans to upend his entire life here and relocate someplace where the three of them would rarely see each other again. He was asking what Felix planned to do about Rory.

"I wish I knew," he said.

That, for some reason, made him look up at the sky, at a softly winking light he knew was Comet Bob passing overhead. Then he realized he'd just made a wish under that comet. But he wasn't fifteen this time, so it wasn't like Bob was under any obligation to grant it, especially since he'd already granted the one Felix made when he was a kid. Somehow, though, he really, really hoped Bob would grant it. Because this one seemed way more important than the other.

Rory stayed up way past her usual bedtime Monday night for a lot of reasons. Mostly, she was waiting for Felix to finish going up and down his stairs as he dropped box after box of this afternoon's collections of memorabilia into the dumpster in the alley, since, once he was done, she was going to go down there and retrieve the boxes herself. She'd heard him return home from someplace about an hour ago, after spending the evening out—and she told herself she was *not* curious about whether or not he'd been with another woman…then wondered why she would think of a woman he was potentially dating as *another* woman, as if he were stepping out on Rory—followed shortly thereafter by his disposal of his belongings. Clearly, he'd been waiting until this late to cart them out, because he thought she'd be asleep by now and not hear him.

Did he really think she'd believed him when he promised her he'd keep everything she begged him to keep? Pshaw. Someday, she knew, he was going to regret throwing away all those wonderful memories, and on that day, she would be able to go into the storage room of Wallflowers where she planned to stash them and say, *Ta-da! Look, Felix! They're all here, safe and sound for you!* Because that was what friends did for each other.

At least, she was pretty sure that was what friends did for each other. And she was kind of starting to think of Felix as a friend. Even though there had been that extremely weird moment earlier in the day when it had seemed like he was going to kiss her. And, even weirder, when she had actually hoped he would. She shouldn't be going around kissing anyone right now. For all she knew, there was someone out there in the world to whom she was already emotionally—and possibly even legally—attached.

And speaking of friends, she hurried her mind along before she could think about that moment of the potential kiss any more than she already had, because she was pretty sure remembering that was another reason she was staying up way past her bedtime, since she couldn't stop thinking about how mouthwatering Felix had looked in his tight tank top and battered jeans, his dark golden hair tumbling forward over amber eyes encircled by thick dark lashes, and how, as she stared at him, wondering what he was going to do next, a single rivulet of perspiration trickled from his temple, to his jaw, to his neck, to settle in the enticing divot at the base of his throat, so that all she wanted to do was reach out and gently thumb it away, then lean forward and run her mouth along the strong column of his neck, tracing his lower lip with her tongue before covering his mouth with hers and dragging her other hand down the length of his sternum, along his flat torso, to the top button of his jeans, and then—

Um, where was she? Besides thinking about almost-kisses and getting unbelievably hot all of a sudden? Wow, she'd had no idea September nights could be so unseasonably warm.

Oh, yeah. She'd been thinking about friends. Like the one whose quinceañera she had attended. The one whose name she couldn't remember. And whose likeness she couldn't remember. And whose anything she couldn't remember. Why could Rory remember being at a party but not the person who threw it? How could she recall the sounds and smells and tastes around her, but not the most important thing—her friend? What was it going to take to produce one concrete memory that would allow her to pinpoint something about herself that might lead to her finally knowing her identity? How much longer was she going to just sit around, twiddling her thumbs, waiting for her brain to be generous enough to throw out some tiny detail that ended up being helpful?

She heard Felix outside, carrying another load down to the dumpster. That made, what? Three trips now? She tried to remember how many boxes he'd had stacked by the door on her way out earlier that he'd promised he was going to take into the restaurant's storage room next to his apartment. Four, she thought. She was pretty sure there had been four. One more trip and he'd be done.

Four boxes full of memories that he was just going to throw away, she marveled again. Literally throw away. How could he do that? She would have given anything to have even one box of memories to call her own. She recalled again the vision she'd had that afternoon of wearing a frilly pink party dress and how vivid had been her conviction that she would never, under normal circumstances, wear something so full of glitter and lace. How the high heels—all one-and-a-half inches of them—had made it so hard for her to navigate, she'd kicked them off to dance. She had obviously not been the kind of girl who went for the traditional feminine trappings of sparkles and showy accessories. So how had she turned into a woman who would be wearing sequins and lamé the night she had her accident?

Just who the hell was she? And why couldn't she remember?

Felix's door squealed open for the fourth time that night, and she listened as he tossed the last of his boxes into the dumpster then climbed the stairs again. She'd give him a half hour to shower and get into bed, then another to fall asleep. Good thing she was nowhere near being sleepy herself. Good thing she was being way too distracted tonight by thoughts about Felix's strong neck and sternum and torso and jeans buttons and—

And maybe she should fix herself a martini. Yeah, that was the ticket.

She'd turned off all the lights beyond her bedroom, so her apartment was dark as she made her way through it. There was enough light coming through the front windows from the streetlamp outside that she didn't need to turn any on to find her way. She reached the kitchen with no problem and even made her martini without incident, then headed back for her bedroom. As she passed through her living room, though, close enough to the open windows to see the street outside, she caught a glimpse of movement and halted before arriving at the rectangle of yellow light spilling in from her bedroom.

There it was again. A shadow in the alley across the street, moving from one side to the other. A brief flash of three shiny gold stripes appeared for a split second at what would be about shoulder height on a man. But not just any man. Tracksuit Guy. She'd know the Adidas trio of sleeve stripes anywhere.

What was he doing out so late? The only time anyone on Water Street saw him was during regular business hours. But it was nearly 2:00 a.m. There was nothing open, and any comet-related festivities had ended hours ago. So what was he doing out there? Across from her shop? No, her shop was closed. What was he doing across from her *home*?

He had to be watching her. Could it be possible he was someone from her past who knew her? Was he someone she knew herself? And if he was, why hadn't he approached her to say hello?

Maybe because her past wasn't the kind where people just came out of the shadows and said howdy-do. Maybe because her past was one where people were way more comfortable staying in the shadows instead.

Rory stood motionless for a good five minutes, waiting to see if he would do something. She was hesitant to leave her apartment to go downstairs for Felix's things as long as Tracksuit Guy was out there, even if he was on the opposite side of the street. Should she call the police? Would they be able to do anything about a guy who was just standing around doing nothing, even if it was in the middle of the night? Or should she just wait him out?

She was still weighing her options when her nighttime visitor finally exited the alley and started heading down the street, whistling softly, as if he hadn't a care in the world. The tune was familiar, but she wasn't quite sure how. Then, like a burst of lightning, the lyrics erupted in her head, and she knew.

The song he was whistling was "*Fly Me to the Moon*." And the version in her head was being sung by Frank Sinatra. Someone who was close to her loved Sinatra and used to sing that song all the time. Someone older. Someone…male? Her father? Why did Rory think her father had liked Sinatra? How could she think that, when she couldn't even remember if she had a father?

She watched Tracksuit Guy as he wandered down the street, perfectly recalling the words to the song he was whistling as if she heard it every day. When he was out of sight and earshot, she moved to her sofa and sat down, trying to concentrate. She was sure it was her father who loved Sinatra. But who was he? And who was her mother? She tried hard—so hard—to pick up an image of the woman who must have raised her.

Why couldn't she remember?

She enjoyed a generous taste of her martini,

closed her eyes and tried to relax. Maybe her brain just needed a little oil for its rusty cogs. She took another sip. Then another. Then she set the glass on her coffee table and leaned back, trying to empty her brain. She sang the words to "Fly Me to the Moon" in her head, hearing Sinatra's voice as if it were coming from the radio right this minute, and—

The radio. Or maybe a CD player. She didn't have a radio or CD player. But that was how she was remembering Frank. She was carried back to her dream of being in the back seat of a big car with a big man behind the wheel. Now he was singing along with Frank, a big booming baritone that filled the vehicle. *In other words, please be true. In other words...*

Here, he glanced back over his shoulder, and she could almost, almost see his face.

...I love you.

Tears sprang to Rory's eyes. Someone had loved her when she was a little girl. She had a family out there somewhere. Why couldn't she remember them?

And then the man was talking to her, reminding her that someone named Paolo would be picking her up after school and to not forget the sweater she left behind yesterday. And he called her a name, but it wasn't like a real name. It was...

Topolina. He called her Topolina. And even in her hazy-minded state, she knew that meant "little mouse." Only it didn't mean "little mouse" in Spanish. It meant "little mouse" in Italian.

She concentrated harder, trying to remember if she knew anything else in Italian. To her surprise, a handful of words and phrases swam up into her brain. But nothing major—nothing conversational. Somehow, she knew she was no more fluent in Italian than she was in Spanish. How did Rory know *some* Italian, in addition to *some* Spanish but clearly be neither of those things? And who was the big man driving the car—her father, she was sure of that—who loved her?

Who the hell *was* she?

She opened her eyes and muttered a few choice words of frustration under her breath. Her brain had clearly given her everything it intended to give her tonight. Maybe tomorrow, she could conjure a few more images. She remembered the boxes she needed to retrieve from the dumpster outside. Felix ought to be out like a light anytime now, then she could head downstairs. At least there would be some memories she could save tonight. If not her own, at least she would keep his safe.

Felix arrived home after dark Tuesday night feeling as if he'd been carrying around a backpack full of bricks all day. No, two backpacks full of bricks. Or even ten. Frankly, he would have rather been doing that than what he'd really spent the day doing—looking for a lost little boy who'd wandered into two hundred acres of woods with his puppy sometime during the night. And not just any little boy. It had been his friend Chance's six-year-old nephew, Finn, who'd only arrived in Endicott a couple of days ago.

Felix still wasn't sure what had possessed the kid to wander off the way he had, but when he'd received a frantic call from Chance early that morning, he'd immediately notified Tinima to tell her she was in charge of La Mariposa that day, then took off for his friend's house. Hell, half the town had headed to Chance's house. Felix and Max had eventually found Finn that afternoon, and he was doing fine now, but wow. Felix had had no idea that fear and panic could exhaust a person to this point. Added to the fact that he was pretty sure he'd covered all two hundred acres of those woods—possibly twice—Felix needed sleep right now like he'd never needed it before.

He was still covered with the sweat and grime of the day, and at this point, he wanted only to shower and fall into bed. He didn't even feel like checking in on how things had gone today at La Mariposa. Hell, Tinima was going to be running the place entirely once Felix left Endicott. He was sure she'd done just fine.

He parked in his designated spot beneath the streetlight behind the restaurant, then unfolded himself from the car with a groan. Every muscle in his body hurt. He must have hiked fifteen miles today. Yeah, bed was sounding better and better. But as he approached the stairs to his apartment, Rory stepped out of the backdoor of Wallflowers, catching him off guard enough that he halted midstride. She should have closed up shop hours ago.

"'Bout time you showed up," she said with a half-hearted smile. Then she must have realized what kind of condition he was in. "Everything okay?"

"It is now," he said. He quickly explained what had happened, then reassured her all was well.

She nodded, but still looked a little uneasy. Somehow, Felix got the impression there was more to it than belated concern for a little boy. "Any chance you have a minute to talk?" she asked.

He wished he did. But he was in no shape to be able to make sense of much of anything at the moment. There was a sense of urgency in Rory's voice, though, that made him say, "What's up?"

Her uneasiness turned to agitation. She shifted

her weight from one foot to the other, then back again. Finally, she said, "I had some more memories of my past last night. I was up late and looked out my living room window at one point, and I saw Tracksuit Guy in the alley across the street and—"

An alarm bell went off at the back of Felix's brain. "Wait, what? Last night? What time?"

"It was going on two," she told him.

"He's never out that late. What was he doing?"

"Just staring at my place, the way he always does."

"We should tell the police."

"We have told the police. They won't do anything."

"They might if they know he's out there in the middle of the night. No way can he explain that away as shopping or going to comet festival events."

Which was true. Nothing ever happened on Water Street at two in the morning. The whole area was silent by eleven. It was one of the many reasons Felix had always told himself he wanted out of Endicott—to go someplace that had life after dark. Even by eleven, the only place in town with any activity was his restaurant, and that was only because the last of his staff were heading home. The kitchen closed at nine on weeknights.

Stores up and down the block closed by seven. There was absolutely no reason for Tracksuit Guy to be anywhere in the area in the wee small hours of the morning.

"Okay," Rory said, "but I'm weirdly grateful he was there, because he triggered a few more memories for me."

"What kind of memories?"

"When he finally left the alley, he started whistling as he walked down the street, and I recognized the song."

"What was it?"

"'Fly Me to the Moon.' I suddenly remembered a version by Frank Sinatra playing in a car that was taking me to school when I was a little girl. And the guy driving the car was my father. I couldn't see his face, Felix, but on some level, I know he was my father. And on the verse where Frank sings 'I love you,' he turned around in his seat and sang that verse to me. Even though his face was hazy in my head, I knew he was smiling. I knew he…" She faltered for a moment, then rallied. "I knew he loved me."

Felix said nothing, only studied Rory in silence. So she did have a family out there. A family who evidently cared for her. Why hadn't they looked for her? Why hadn't they found her? Then again, maybe they were looking for her. Maybe they were just looking in the wrong place.

"Someone out there loves me, Felix," she said, sounding oddly anxious about the fact. "Or, at least, someone did, once upon a time."

With that statement, too, she sounded kind of strange. As if she were wondering that if someone had loved her as a child, why wouldn't they still love her as an adult?

"There's more," she said.

"What?"

"In addition to some Spanish, I understand some Italian."

With that, things got weirder still. Where had Rory grown up? The United Nations?

"Seriously?" he asked.

She nodded. "I spent a lot of today on the internet, listening to other languages, too, to see if any of them sounded familiar to me, but nothing did. And I listened to more Italian, too, to see if I was fluent. I'm not."

The more Rory learned about herself, the stranger everything got. Instead of helping them find out who she was, what little bits and pieces of knowledge about herself that she'd managed to remember had only made it more difficult to figure out her origins. And if Felix was as confused about all that as he was, he couldn't imagine how frustrated she must be.

"I wish I could help," he told her. "But right now, Rory, I am so brain-dead and exhausted, I don't know what to think or say."

She nodded. "Yeah, I really need to get to bed myself because I got so little sleep last night."

In spite of that, she still looked like she wished the two of them could talk. Felix sympathized. But he was whooped. Any advice or insight he might be able to offer at this point would probably just be the offer of a glass of wine and a sofa to sit on while he nodded off beside her.

"Look," he said, "tomorrow morning, I have to drive up to Indianapolis to see a property I'm thinking about buying. If you want to come with me, we can talk on the way."

His offer brightened her up immediately. Ironic, since he was already wishing he hadn't invited her. He knew he shouldn't spend more time with Rory than he had to. And he especially didn't need to be cooped up with her for hours in a car, where there was no way to escape.

"I'd love to," she said. "Let me double-check with Ezra, to see if he can mind the store while I'm gone, but I'm sure it won't be a problem." She started to turn away, then spun back around. "Thanks, Felix. I really appreciate it."

"No problem," he told her.

She smiled halfheartedly, then headed back into her shop, leaving him wondering yet again how he'd managed to get so pulled back into the past. A past that wasn't even his own, but that somehow made him feel and think about things he hadn't felt or thought in a long time. Things he hadn't wanted to ever feel or think about again.

No problem, he'd told her. Funny, since, suddenly, it felt like every problem he'd ever had was coming home to roost.

Back in her apartment, Rory closed and locked the door behind herself. She really should go to bed. But as exhausted as she was, she knew sleep was still a long way off.

She went to her kitchen and looked at the three-hundred-pound, cold press, acid-free, mold-made rag paper she'd clipped to an easel earlier that evening, then at the collection of watercolor paints beside it. She had no idea how she'd known to buy three-hundred-pound, cold press, acid-free, mold-made rag paper, but she'd gravitated right to it the moment she'd seen it at Arabella's Art Supplies that afternoon. She'd also gravitated immediately toward a specific brand of watercolor paints, then had been disappointed that none of the brushes in stock had been ones she knew she liked. She did somehow recognize the name of one brand, though, so had chosen a set of those.

Then, before leaving work that evening, she'd put together a simple arrangement of fairy foxglove, toadflax, and forget-me-nots in a green glass vase. She smiled at having chosen that last flower, but how could she not? Now the arrangement sat at the center of her kitchen table atop a pale yellow tablecloth, a collection of soft purples and blues complemented by bits of frothy white and silvery greens. A shaft of buttery streetlight tumbled through the kitchen window, giving the flowers an aura of warmth she found beautiful. Since she knew that streetlight often sputtered, its illumination changing from yellow to white to blue, she quickly snapped a photo with her phone, because she wasn't sure yet if she was able to paint from memory.

Of course, she wasn't sure she was able to paint at all. Just because she'd had one quick impression of a painting in a room she couldn't even remember being in didn't mean she was the one who had painted it.

But she was kind of positive that she was.

She inhaled a deep breath and released it slowly, then opened the first of the half-dozen tints she'd purchased, along with an inexpensive plastic palette to mix them. She squeezed a dollop of cerulean into one cavity and ultramarine into another. Black, then white, then a few other odd shades for mixing. Then she went to work. Tentatively at first, then, gradually, with a little more confidence. At one point, she had to bring in an extra lamp because the streetlight went out completely. But even with the night outside her window going black, Rory continued to paint.

And paint pretty well, if she did say so herself.

She knew how to paint, she realized. She'd been right. And she liked to paint flowers. A lot. When had she come to love all things that grew out of the ground? Who had taught her to paint? And why was this something that came almost instinctively, the way so many tasks had for her, when there were other things she struggled so hard to remember?

It was going to happen soon, she thought. She didn't know how she knew that, but her entire life was lurking at the edges of her brain, and it was about to come spilling into focus. She didn't know when or where it would happen, or what would be the impetus to propel it. But it was coming. That much she knew. She just hoped, when it happened, she wasn't appalled and repulsed at what it turned out to be.

Chapter Eight

There wasn't a more boring drive anywhere than through rural Indiana, Felix thought as he and Rory made the trip to Indianapolis the next morning. All corn, all the time, and a horizon as flat as a *tostone*. Only thirty minutes into the roughly two-hour excursion, and he was already missing the hilly knobs of the southern part of the state. Which was weird, because he'd never missed Endicott in his life, had welcomed any chance to escape, and had always resented it when it was time to go home.

He told himself his unrest was due to the fact that Rory was with him. Today's trip was one he'd planned on making alone—he hadn't even told Chance or Max about it. Yeah, they knew he wanted to branch out and open restaurants outside their hometown, but he hadn't explicitly told them he was planning on leaving, too, or when he was planning to do it. He still wasn't sure how they were going to take the news of his relocation. The three of them had been pretty much a unit since they were kids. Sure, they were each living their own lives now, but not a week went by that they didn't still get together in some form or another. And they all knew they had each other's backs, no matter what trouble might come, or when. If Felix was living hours—or even days—away, how was he going to be there for his friends at the drop of a hat? How were they going to be there for him?

He shook the questions off. He didn't have to think about that right now. Not when there were so many other things to unsettle him. Things like juggling more than one restaurant at a time. And all the ins and outs of moving from one place to another. And where, exactly, he eventually wanted to end up. He'd been making plans for this expansion for almost two years. Why weren't they crystalizing better than they were? Why was his business plan still so much more *plan* than it was *business*?

"Felix?"

It was the first time Rory had spoken since they merged onto the interstate. He'd halfway thought she'd dozed off, thanks to their 6:00-a.m. departure. But he wanted to be back at the restaurant before the lunch crowd got out of hand. She'd been half asleep when she met him at his place. They'd stopped long enough to fill the gas tank and grab a couple of coffees, but she'd barely touched hers. And they hadn't had breakfast at all.

"I'm getting hungry," she told him apologetically.

He'd hoped the coffee would tide them over until they made it to Indy, but he had to admit his stomach was growling, too. Unfortunately, unless they wanted to pull over for a couple ears of corn, it could be a while.

"We just passed an exit," he said. "I'm not sure how far it is to the next one, or if it will have decent food."

"Even a bag of powdered doughnuts from a mini-mart would be fine," she told him.

He couldn't quite hide his wince in response. She laughed.

"I know, I know," she said. "I'm not the gourmet you are."

He had to tread carefully here. "It's not that," he said.

"Yes, it is."

"Okay, it is that. I mean…powdered doughnuts? Really?"

"They're not that different from La Mariposa's pastelitos."

"¡Muerdete la lengua!"

She laughed again. "Hey, I understood that! But I won't bite my tongue. Sweet pastries are sweet pastries. So there."

"That's the last time I bring you anything from the restaurant for free," he said. "From now on, you pay your own way, *yuma*."

"Okay, *yuma* is a Spanish word I don't understand. You've called me that twice now. What does it mean?"

"I think maybe only Cubans use it," he said. "It means anyone who's not from Cuba, basically. Or from any Spanish-speaking place."

She leaned her elbow on the window ledge and watched him thoughtfully. "Yeah, okay, that's fair. I think we've safely ruled out that I'm not from Cuba. And now that I realize I know some Italian, it's probably safe to say I'm not Hispanic at all."

"Probably not," he agreed.

"But I only know a little Italian, so I must not be from Italy."

"True, but there are a lot of Italian Americans in the States."

"Probably not all that many in Indiana, though."

"Maybe in Indianapolis," he said. "And you were found in Gary, which is near Chicago. There are probably a lot of Italian American communities up there."

"It's possible," she said, her voice edged with something akin to unease. "But my social worker drove me around Gary and Chicago both, to see if anything jarred any memories, and nothing did. I mean, Chicago did make me feel..."

"What?" he asked when she didn't finish.

"Unpleasant," she said. It was a word that could mean a lot of things. "Something may have happened to me in Chicago, but I don't think I'm from there. Or Gary, for that matter." She sat up straighter and gazed out the window at the endless agricultural landscape. "In fact, something tells me I'm not from Indiana at all. I don't think I'm from anyplace where there's a lot of farmland."

"That rules out a lot of states, then. Most of them have a lot of agriculture of some kind between cities."

"Yeah, I guess so..."

"Maybe New England or the Pacific Northwest," he suggested. "There's mostly woodlands between cities in those areas."

"Or the Southwest," she suggested further.

"Mostly desert there. I've thought about all those areas, actually. But I've google-imaged places all over the country since my amnesia, to see if anyplace looked familiar. No place did."

She threw out the word *amnesia* so casually, Felix noted. He still stumbled over it even when he had to think about it. Of course, she'd lived with it for months now. Maybe she was getting used to it. Which was a pretty awful thing to have to get used to.

An idea popped into his head. "Okay, let's try this," he said. "It was something fun we used to do on the bus to school when we got bored. Word association."

She smiled. "I did that with one of my therapists at the hospital," she said. "And I did very well with associating things like 'hot' and 'cold' and 'up' and 'down.'"

"Oh, come on. Those are easy. Let's try something more challenging."

"What? Like you say, 'pastelitos,' and I say, 'powdered doughnuts'?"

He chuckled. "No. Like..." He thought for a moment. "We'll start with something simple then get creative. So if I say, 'yellow,' you say..."

"Blue," she replied.

"I say, 'cat,' you say..."

"Dog."

"Light."

"Dark. Felix, I've already done all these," she told him. "It wasn't helpful."

"Okay, gimme a minute to think of some weird ones."

She expelled a sound of vague annoyance. "Fine."

He thought for a minute, thinking back on their conversations, focusing on the occasions when she'd actually experienced some kind of memories. Finally, he conjured a half-dozen words he thought might help. He could start off with the easy ones, then get into some that might be more challenging, or even uncomfortable for her.

"Music," he said. He thought she would reply with something they'd already covered, like Sinatra or reggaeton.

Instead, she said, "Rock 'n' roll."

Fair enough. Still, it kind of surprised him. It was an interesting enough answer that he decided to take a momentary side route from his original line of questioning.

"Books," he said.

"*To Kill a Mockingbird*," she replied immediately.

Which she had mentioned before that she had recognized, so not too helpful after all.

"Movies," he said.

When she didn't reply right away, he gave her

a quick glance and saw her staring through the windshield with an expression of something akin to wistfulness.

"Rory?" he prodded her.

She looked at him. Then she smiled. "*Cinderella*," she said softly. "The old, animated one. It just popped into my head. I think it was the first movie I ever saw—" before he could say anything, she hurried on "—and I'm pretty sure my grandmother took me. I don't remember her, but somehow, I know she was the one who took me to see it. I even remember some of the songs."

At that she started humming something he didn't recognize. Then she started singing, "A dream is a wish your heart makes..." with the most whimsical smile he'd ever seen. Then she closed her eyes and went on about some stuff with sleep and dreams and wishes and heartaches, and Felix figured that was just as good a prompt as any he was going to get. The minute she finished, he fired off another round of words.

"Wish," he said.

With her eyes still closed, she replied, "A horse for my tenth birthday. Then my eleventh. Then my twelfth. Then my thirteenth."

Wow. He couldn't believe this was working.

"Dream," he continued.

"To play for the WNBA when I grow up."

It didn't escape his notice how the few memories she managed to recall seemed to center a lot more frequently on her childhood than her adulthood. It was…interesting.

"Family," he said.

Eyes still closed, she shook her head and didn't reply.

He tried again. "Happiness."

Now she smiled again. "Peonies."

The words he'd thought would be good ones to try were shriveling up now because his hunger was overtaking him. So he blurted out, "Pancakes."

She laughed and replied, "Diner."

Oh, that really was interesting. He would have said something like *waffles* or *syrup*.

He was running out of ideas, so looked around. Corn. Sky. Interstate. "I-65," he said, just throwing it out because why not?

"I-95," she replied instantly. Then her eyes flew open, and she looked shocked. "Why did I say I-95? Where's I-95? I might be from someplace it goes through."

"Got me," Felix said. "Google it."

She snatched her phone from her bag and did just that. "It runs from Miami all the way through Maine," she said. "Well, that's not helpful."

"Of course it is," he told her. "It narrows things down to the East Coast."

"Oh, sure. It only goes through one, two, three..." She continued to count silently. "Only like a dozen states for us to choose from."

"Well, you don't have much of an accent, so we can probably rule out the ones in the Deep South and a lot of New England."

"It's still like a needle in a haystack."

Felix disagreed. If she was from somewhere along I-95, that ruled out like 75 percent of the country.

"It's a start," he told her. "And maybe it'll jog something else."

He was going to suggest continuing the word association, going state by state to see if anything else popped into her brain, but an exit sign came into view with an advertisement for a fast-food chain he could stomach reasonably well.

"We can grab some breakfast at the next exit," he said. "Not that there will be any diners there," he added.

"I did say, 'diner,' didn't I?" she said. "That must mean the Northeast. They don't have diners anywhere else, do they?"

"Not in big quantities," he said, "but there are still some scattered around. We have Deb's

Downtown Diner in Endicott. So it's possible there was one you frequented someplace else."

It was still so odd to him that she seemed to have such a wealth of general knowledge, even when she couldn't remember specifics about herself. Amnesia was weird, he thought, not for the first time. How could the brain retain so many memories of the world at large and how things worked in general, but not who a person was or where they were from?

"And I really did want a horse for my birthday when I was a kid," she continued. "I remember that now."

"Did you ever get one?"

She thought for a minute, then shook her head again. "I don't think so."

"And playing for the WNBA when you grew up," he reminded her with a grin. "That's quite the aspiration." Not that she wasn't tall enough. "You must have played basketball for your school or something, if that was what you wanted to do. I played in high school," he added. "You and I should shoot some hoops when we get back. See how good you really are."

She grinned back. "That would fun. I wouldn't mind finding that out for myself."

"It's a date then," Felix said without thinking.

Quickly, he added, "I mean...not a *date*. Just, you know, a date."

"I get it," she assured him.

But she looked a little disappointed. He told himself it was probably because she wanted to continue the word game, too, to see if it stirred anything else. It was still a long drive to Indy. They could maybe try again after they ate. Maybe their brains would work even better then.

Her memory did seem to be returning to her, though, little by little. Maybe, before long, she really would remember who she was and where she was from. And then she could return to the place where she belonged and the people who loved her. She could finally find her place in the world outside of Endicott, just like Felix planned to do.

The thought should have brought him comfort on both their behalf. Instead, for some reason, it made him feel even more restless.

Breakfast, he told himself. He needed food. That was the cure-all for everything.

Rory stood with Felix and his Indianapolis Realtor in the kitchen of the restaurant he was looking to buy, wondering why she was trying to assess the place when she had no idea what his—or anyone's—needs were when it came to buying a restaurant. Which meant she could strike *working at a restaurant* off her list of things that weren't a part of her past. Yay. Only eight billion more to go.

They had resumed the word association game after grabbing breakfast, but it hadn't been as successful as their first attempt. Maybe there was something about being half asleep and hungry that had allowed her brain to release more information. Might not be a bad idea to try another time under similar circumstances. She did seem to remember more when she was thinking about or doing something besides trying to remember things. She'd see what Felix thought.

Felix, whom she was becoming more and more reliant on when it came to retrieving her memories. Felix, who seemed more and more insistent on keeping her at arm's length. Which she should have considered a good thing, since getting closer to him was the last thing she should be thinking about. Especially when she didn't even know what lurked in her real life. The real life that was creeping closer and closer all the time.

So why did she keep thinking about getting closer to Felix? And why did the thought of him leaving town feel so wrong?

She pushed the thought away—again—and focused on the matter at hand. Frankly, she wasn't all that impressed with the property. The kitchen was certainly bigger than the one at La Mariposa, but it was more run-down. The appliances looked old, even to her untrained eye, and there were stains on the ceiling and tiles missing from the floor. The dining room, too, was larger, but it was dingy and dark and smelled of burned onions.

She knew he could fix it up, and it could probably be as charming as the La Mariposa he ran now. But this one would be situated downtown, on the street level of a glass-and-steel office tower, with cars and buses zipping by outside and the glitter of more glass and steel across the street. The location was the antithesis of a small-town Main Street, and somehow that made it feel like it would be less authentic than Felix's current place.

It didn't feel like Felix, either. As often as he insisted how much he disliked having grown up in a small town, and as often as he emphasized his desire to go someplace big and bold and busy, he really didn't strike her as the metropolitan type. Did he realize how difficult it was to move someplace, especially someplace so much bigger, where he didn't know anyone and had no support system? There was a lot to be said for having roots somewhere. She knew that, because she didn't have roots herself.

"It's not bad," he said now, running his hand

along the stainless steel hood over the stove. He grimaced, though, when he pulled his hand away and found it covered with brown…goo. "Needs a major cleaning and some cosmetic work, but the bones are good. It could work."

"The location is awesome," his Realtor, a tidy young man in a brown suit named Yusef, assured him. "The previous owner always had a full house for lunch during the week."

"How was the dinner and weekend crowd?"

Here Yusef's smile faltered a little. "Well, he didn't really try to attract a dinner or weekend clientele."

Even Rory could tell he was trying to avoid saying there wasn't anyone around here any other time of the day or week.

"But Downtown Indy is still super busy in the evenings and on weekends," he hurried to reassure Felix.

"Sure, in some areas," Felix agreed. "But this area is mostly financial. The nearest bar is two blocks west. And the only other restaurant on this block is another one that's obviously catering to the lunch crowd."

"So then nighttime parking wouldn't be a problem for your diners," Yusef said hopefully.

Felix threw him an almost convincing smile. "Lemme look around a little more."

"Of course," the Realtor said just as his phone rang. "Excuse, me, I need to take this. I'll just be a minute."

"Take your time," Felix told him.

As Yusef wandered off, Felix took one final look at the kitchen, then meandered back toward the dining room. Rory followed, trying to see the place through his eyes. But all she saw was a tired-looking establishment past its prime. Even with paint and new furnishings, she just couldn't see the place coming to life. Certainly not with the heart and soul that La Mariposa had.

He spun around to look at her. "What do you think?" he asked.

"How would I know what to think?" she replied. "I have no idea what goes into making a successful restaurant."

"Yeah, but how does it *feel* to you?"

She was reluctant to answer honestly, because she didn't want to dash any hopes he might have of buying the place. Hers was just one woman's opinion. One woman who didn't even have much to compare the space to.

When she didn't say anything, he asked, "If you lived in the burbs, would you come downtown on the weekend just to visit one restaurant?"

"Depends on the restaurant, I guess."

"Fair enough. If you lived downtown, would you make the walk five or six blocks?"

She lifted her shoulders and let them drop. "I'm not much of a foodie, Felix, so I personally probably wouldn't make any special trips. If it was convenient to my job, I might come in after work."

He looked resigned. "Yeah, that's my thought, too. I mean, I do have a handful of customers who drive down to Endicott from Indianapolis just to eat at La Mariposa, so I'm sure I could count on them, at least."

"If people make special trips that far, then you probably could lure people into this part of town on the nights and weekends," she told him. "Especially if there's some event going on that they could attend afterward."

Rory didn't think she'd ever been to Indianapolis and was frankly surprised by how big it was once they arrived. It wasn't Chicago by any stretch, but it was still big. Probably twice the size of Louisville, across the river from Endicott. Not surprisingly, the city didn't rouse any kind of familiarity in her, as much as she'd kind of hoped it would. But the neighborhood where the restaurant was located could have been any street in any urban area in any place in the country. Maybe that was another reason she didn't feel like it was suited to La Mariposa. Or to Felix. It was just too…common.

"Yeah, maybe…" he said in response to her remark.

She hesitated before saying what else she wanted to say. But she felt like she needed to say it. Finally, she told him, "Felix, I'm not sure this is the right place for another La Mariposa."

He looked at her, but didn't seem surprised by her comment. Even so, he asked, "Why not?"

She had no idea. She'd only ever been in Felix's restaurant a few times, to deliver his flower order for the day, or to see if someone had change for a hundred-dollar bill or whatever. But she'd always found it charming the moment she entered, full of soft, multicolored pastel walls and bright Cuban artwork, from oil paintings of street life to vintage cars made of papier-mâché to carved wooden saints. And playing over it all, soft acoustic guitar and a singer who always sounded melancholy.

It was cozy. Friendly. Intimate. Walking into La Mariposa felt like going home. Even to someone like Rory, who didn't even know where home was. Honestly, she wasn't sure Felix would be able to create that atmosphere anywhere but Endicott. But trying to explain that to him…

"It just doesn't feel like La Mariposa," she said.

Strangely, he seemed to understand, because

he nodded. "Yeah, I'm not sure it's a good fit, either. Maybe I should look for something in the suburbs."

Maybe. But that didn't quite feel right, either.

Yusef rejoined them then, apologizing again for his phone call and asking Felix what he wanted to do.

"I'm not sure it's going to work," he told the Realtor.

"Well, keep it in mind," the other man said.

Felix promised he would, but Rory was pretty sure he'd already dismissed it. She felt strangely relieved. And not just because the place didn't feel right for La Mariposa, she realized. But also because, for now, Felix would be staying put in Endicott. She knew it was a mistake for her to think that way, knew it was ridiculous for her to want him to be close. Number one, he'd made clear he had no intention of staying close. Number two, he'd made clear he wasn't the kind of man to get involved with any woman for long. And number three, he'd made clear he didn't want to get involved with Rory specifically.

Why that was, she still wasn't sure. But she told herself to be grateful for it. She didn't need to be getting involved with a man like Felix, either—in general or specifically. Although she was reasonably certain now she wasn't a married woman—the thought of that just didn't feel right, the way so many things she'd considered over the past few days didn't feel right—she still had no idea for certain what kind of things lay in her past. She wasn't sure she'd be staying in Endicott, either, if she regained her memory. *When* she regained her memory, she amended, since she was starting to retrieve dribs and drabs of it, so surely the rest would be coming through soon.

But playing for the WNBA? she asked herself when she recalled the memory that had floated into her brain earlier. Wanting a horse for her birthday? Did she still want those things? Somehow, she didn't think she did. But what had happened to change her mind about that? When had she gone from a horse-loving athlete who hated lacy, girly dresses to a woman with a mass of highlighted hair and hot-pink nail polish, wearing what she'd been wearing the night of her accident?

Just who the hell was she, really?

Chapter Nine

"Okay, so, clearly, neither of us has played basketball for a while now."

Felix lay on his back beside Rory, both of them panting hard, in the middle of the basketball court in Kickapoo Park, where he and Max and Chance had spent way too much of their summers growing up. It was late—the sun had set midway through their game—and the sky above them was nearly black, save for the glare of the buzzing streetlamps located at each corner of the court keeping the edges of the darkness a hazy white. And the lights, he knew, would be going off soon, because the park closed at eleven.

"It might have been a while," Rory said, "but neither of us has forgotten how to play the game."

This was true. Like riding a bicycle, school sports evidently stayed with a person forever. Too bad their school stamina didn't. He should have figured that would be the case when he challenged her that morning. But Rory had obviously played ball at some point in her life, because she'd given Felix as good a game as he'd ever had, and their one-on-one had ended in a full-on tie. He hadn't yielded her an inch, had played the same way he would have played with any guy from his old team who might have challenged him. And she'd returned in kind.

Now they were both breathing hard, their shorts and T-shirts drenched with sweat. Felix's damp hair clung to his forehead, and when he turned his head to look at Rory, he saw her cropped dark tresses glistening.

"Wonder who you played for?" he said. "Was it high school or college? Or, hey, maybe you really did make it to the WNBA."

She chuckled. "If I'd played professionally, I would have kicked your ass."

He laughed, too. "Good point."

All four streetlamps on the court suddenly clicked loudly, then went dark. The buzz that had been serenading them all night went silent, and they were enveloped in darkness and quiet.

"That can't be good," Rory said ominously.

"It's fine. It must be eleven. The park just closed."

"Should we clear out?"

"Nah. No one ever enforces it. Kids come here all the time after hours."

"Should we at least move from the courts? Are they going to want to play ball?"

Felix folded an arm to tuck it between the asphalt and his head and turned to look at her again. "They don't come here after hours to play ball, Rory."

She looked back at him, confused for a minute. Then she said, *"Oooh."*

"Yeah, *oooh*," he repeated.

She grinned. "Did you do that when you were a kid?"

He grinned back. "Maybe."

"Romeo," she charged.

"*Mmm*, I prefer to think of it as just having lots and lots of charisma."

"Right."

He looked up at the sky again. "Besides, this is the best place in Endicott to comet watch. It's a big park, and we're far enough away from town that, once the lights go out, you can see all kinds of stars. And, of course, Bob."

Rory looked up, too. "Right. The comet. Where is it?"

"He," Felix said. "Bob has always been a he."

"Comets have genders?"

"This one does."

"Is he actually named Comet Bob?"

He could hear the smile in her voice. He supposed it was kind of funny, a comet named Bob. But that was how he'd always been known, for as long as Felix could remember.

Even so, he told her, "No. He was named after some Eastern European astronomer who discovered him. But the guy's name is like fifty letters long and has more consonants than vowels."

"Somehow, though, I bet you know his full name," Rory said, smiling.

Felix smiled back. "Bobrzynyckolonycki."

She nodded. "Comet Bob it is."

"Yeah, that's who he's always been to us."

"Where is he?" she asked again.

Felix searched the sky and found him immediately. "There," he said, pointing.

"Where?"

"Do you see the Big Dipper?"

"Yeah."

Again, he wondered how she could recall

something like that, which she'd obviously learned in school the same way he had, but not her own name.

"See where the handle of the Big Dipper starts to bend?" he said. "Follow that past the last star in the handle about three inches, till you see a white thing a little bigger than the stars."

"That's Bob?"

"That's Bob."

"And he comes around every fifteen years?"

"Like clockwork."

"So you were fifteen the last time he came around."

"Yep."

He looked at Rory again. Even in the darkness, he could see she was holding back a chuckle. "What's so funny?"

"I'm just trying to picture you at fifteen," she told him. "I mean, if I was going to my friend's quinceañera then, hating my scratchy froufy dress and heels, what were you doing? Besides luring unsuspecting girls into the park with your copious amounts of charisma, I mean."

Now Felix was the one to chuckle. Not so much at her charisma comment, but at the irony of her question, once he realized the answer. "You won't believe me," he said.

"Sure I will."

"This time fifteen years ago, I was here, lying in almost this exact same spot."

"You were not."

"Oh, yes, I was. One night and a few hours from now. Around two a.m."

"You were comet-watching?" she guessed.

He made himself admit the truth to her. "Okay, okay. I came here to meet Mary Alice Doherty, who was also supposed to sneak out that night."

"Aha!" Rory said with a laugh. "I knew it."

"It wasn't what you think," he said. Well, not entirely. Sure he'd been looking forward to some decent making out. But before that—

"We came here to make a wish."

Damn. He hadn't meant to reveal that last part.

"But she stood me up," he hastily added, hoping Rory would jump on the opportunity for some kind of *I told you so* instead of asking him about the wishing thing.

No such luck.

"A wish?" she asked.

He sighed with resolution. "Yeah. A wish."

She turned on her side to look at him, lifting her upper body and bending an elbow to rest her head in her hand. His eyes had adjusted to the darkness by now, so he could see her fairly clearly in the moon- and starlight. And, as always, he was struck by how beautiful she was by simply *being*.

No makeup, no fussy hair, wearing a sweaty T-shirt and shorts. There weren't many people, male or female, who could be that appealing without trying. Even he had to take some pains to look his best every day.

But Rory? She was appealing just by existing. No, she was more than appealing. She was—

"Why were you making a wish?" she asked, thankfully sidetracking him before he could finish that thought.

"Because that's what you do when you're fifteen years old in Endicott if you were born here in a year when Bob comes around—which I was. You make a wish upon his return when you're fifteen. That's what the legend says to do."

"Bob has a legend, too?"

"Oh, Bob has lots of legends," he assured her. "Like how he creates cosmic disturbances while he's visiting that make people do things they would normally never do."

Her smile broadened. "Oh, this is going to be good. Like what?"

Felix looked at the sky again, because looking at Rory was making him think and feel things he had no business thinking or feeling. *Thanks a lot, Bob*, he told the comet silently. *Just turn all the fables I'm about to tell Rory into facts, why don't you?*

"I've heard all kinds of things over the years," he told her. "Like how, last time Bob came around, people were quitting their jobs to follow their dreams and completely changing the styles of clothes they wore and making up with family members they hadn't spoken to for decades and falling in love with people they had no business falling in love with."

"Ooh, ooh. You have to tell me more about that last one. That's like a Hallmark movie waiting to happen."

Felix really didn't want to go into specifics about stuff like that—not when Bob was already messing with his head in that regard. But Rory seemed to be enjoying the stories. So he decided to tell her what he'd heard about the comet's last appearance.

"Supposedly, last time Bob was here, there was this one woman who fell in love with a mobster who came to town. And there was this other couple who had been sworn enemies since high school who ended up getting married. Another woman who everyone said was destined to be an old maid ended up with some international playboy no one ever thought would settle down. That kind of thing."

"Wow."

"Yeah. Probably none of it is true. Sounds like

the stuff of fiction to me. Anyway, like I said, if you're born the year Bob comes around, you make a wish when he comes again, when you're fifteen. Then, when he comes back a third time, when you're thirty, that wish is supposed to come true."

She looked delighted by this information. "So that means your wish is going to come true this year! What did you wish for?"

At the time, he'd been wishing not for some-*one* to come along and turn his life upside down. But for some*thing* to happen that would send his life in a new direction. But he was beginning to think maybe Bob had gotten a little confused about that.

With much reluctance, he admitted, "I wished for something *interesting* to happen in Endicott."

Her expression soured. "That's it? That's what you wished for? Something interesting to happen?"

"What's so bad about that?"

"You could've wished for a million dollars or something."

"No, that was Chance's wish," Felix said.

Her mouth dropped open. "Are you serious?"

"Yeah."

"Did he get it?"

It honestly hadn't occurred to Felix until that

moment that Chance's wish of fifteen years ago had, in fact, come true this year. In a way.

"Sorta?" he told her. "I mean, he doesn't have it yet, but it's kind of on its way?"

She shook her head, but smiled again. "What did your friend Max wish for?"

Chance smiled back. "Pretty much a second chance with his high school crush."

"And how's that going?"

Chance looked up at Bob again and grinned. "Let's just say it's not going quite the way Max hoped it would. But the week's not over yet," he hastened to add. There was still a good chance Marcy Hanlon—now la comtesse Marcella Robillard—would come around.

"And you wished for something interesting to happen," Rory echoed. "Which, you have to admit, a next-door neighbor with amnesia kind of is."

"Yeah, but that wasn't what I was really wishing for," he said.

Her smile fell.

"No, I mean, I was actually wishing for an event, not a person."

Wow. That came out even worse.

"No, I get it," she said, almost sounding convincing. "That's valid. And I guess, when you get down to it, amnesia is something that's bizarre and awful and sad more than it is interesting."

"Rory, that's not true. You're misunderstanding."

She jumped up and brushed off the back of her shorts. "Nah, it's fine. We should probably get going. It's getting late."

Yeah, it was getting late, Felix thought. But where she was probably talking about the hour of day, he couldn't help thinking it was getting late for other things, too. Things like feeling the way he was beginning to feel about Rory. When that was the last thing he could afford to be doing.

They made the drive back to town in pretty much total silence. Rory told herself it was because she was exhausted. Between getting up earlier than usual that morning and sleeping so little last night, then driving to Indianapolis and back, then working, the rest of the day and playing basketball so late in the evening, of course she would be beat. But the fatigue she was feeling now went deeper than skin or even bone deep. It was soul deep.

She supposed she shouldn't be surprised that, after her wordplay with Felix, so many forgotten relics had emerged from her brain. They'd tried again on the drive home, and she'd unearthed more disjointed memories. Of herself sitting in a deserted ice cream parlor doing math homework appropriate for a middle-schooler. Of lying in a bedroom where virtually everything was pink, listening to My Chemical Romance while a woman pounded on her bedroom door, yelling for her to turn it down. And she'd remembered driving a car—her first car, she somehow knew, one she received for her sixteenth birthday. A bright blue Mustang convertible that a man out of view was telling her had just rolled off the line.

So if she'd been sixteen when that particular model came out, that meant she was twenty-eight now. Felix had been right with his calculation about her age at the quinceañera. Having that confirmed, finally knowing a concrete thing about herself had sent her reeling, and she'd told Felix she couldn't do the word association anymore.

But her brain hadn't been finished. She'd eventually dozed off on the ride home from Indianapolis, and she'd dreamed about sitting in a different kitchen than the one she'd seen in her mind's eye before, watching a woman with white hair, wearing a flowered dress and apron, stirring something on the stove. That dream had segued into another, one where Rory was at a school locker talking to another girl, but that girl had been behind the open locker door, and Rory hadn't been able to see her face.

Why could she never see anyone's face? She was starting to have so many memories, but never any with distinct faces. Or names. Or locations. How could she be remembering so much and yet still so little?

Felix turned his car down the alley behind their apartments and parked in his designated spot. It was all Rory could do not to jump out and scream her frustration at the universe with every breath she had. Instead, she exited the car wearily and started making her way to the fire escape leading to her door. Belatedly, she turned around to tell Felix good-night, only to find that he was following her instead of heading to his own place.

"You don't have to walk me up," she told him.

"Oh, I think I do," he replied pointedly.

But he wasn't looking at her. He was looking up at her door. She followed his gaze and could see well enough from the hazy streetlight behind them that the outside door to her place was ajar, and the light above—the one she habitually left on at night, whether she was home or away—was broken.

"We should call the police," she said.

He nodded. But instead of doing that, he made his way to the stairs and started climbing them.

"Felix!" she hissed.

"I'm just going to take a quick look."

"They could still be in there."

"Yeah, that's why I want to take a quick look."

She withdrew her phone and dialed 911, told the operator she needed the police, and was immediately transferred to the Endicott PD, where she was promptly put on hold and told that her call was very important to them, and they'd be right with her. By now, Felix was at the top of the fire escape, pulling open the outside door to go in. She knew it wasn't a good idea but, not wanting him to face danger alone, she followed, still on wait with the cops, arriving at the top to find he had entered her place and switched on what lights he could, and was having a look around. When the hold music for the PD started playing "*The Piña Colada Song,*" she decided she didn't care how dangerous the situation might be, no one should be forced to listen to that. So she hung up and followed him inside.

"Whoever broke in is gone," he said. "But it doesn't look like anything was disturbed. At least not in here."

She gave the living room and kitchen a quick once-over. Her MacBook was sitting on the sofa, but it wasn't on the side where she'd left it. It was password protected, but she went to it anyway, to double-check. The prompt was up, asking if she wanted to reset her password using her Apple ID, which meant someone had tried to enter a password three times and been locked out.

"Someone tried to get into my laptop," she told Felix. "But they didn't steal it. How weird."

A ripple of unease went up her spine at the realization that someone had been in her home within the past couple of hours and had been messing with her stuff. She took another hasty look around. Her TV and the used PlayStation she'd bought at the Endicott flea market were still covered by a thin layer of dust—she really should do better with housekeeping—so clearly hadn't been touched. All told, the three items together could have netted someone a couple thousand bucks, so whoever broke in either hadn't been looking to gain monetarily or else was an idiot. And the fact that they'd tried to get onto her computer was an indication the former was the case, not the latter.

"Has anything else been messed with?" Felix asked.

She went to her bedroom. Here, things were clearly amiss, but the room hadn't been ransacked as one would expect a burglar to leave things. Her dresser had clearly been searched—a couple of the drawers were still open, with papers and clothing and whatnot sticking out—and her closet door was agape, the boxes and bags on the top shelf arranged in a way she hadn't left them. Whoever had come in looked to have taken them all down, gone through them, then put them carelessly back in place. She pulled them down herself, to see if any of the contents were missing. It was mostly stuff for work, but there were a few personal items she'd collected since her arrival in Endicott.

Felix entered the room as she was pulling down the last of the boxes. "Is everything okay?" he asked.

"I still don't know," she told him, her unease growing.

It was bad enough that someone had been in her living room. But her bedroom was a much more personal, intimate space. She wasn't even all that comfortable having Felix here. The realization that a total stranger had had their grubby hands all over her stuff made nausea roll through her belly.

"I think everything is here," she finally said. "But someone obviously went through my stuff. They don't seem to have taken anything, though. Why would someone break in and not steal anything?"

Rory thought then about the things in the box

under her bed. She didn't want to pull those out while Felix was here. But she needed to know if they were still there and whether or not her intruder had found them. With much reluctance, she dropped to her knees and pulled out the box. She knew before she opened it that her visitor had indeed discovered her secret stash, because the lid was askew. She opened it anyway. Inside, the garments lay in a way that indicated clearly they'd been manhandled. She withdrew them one by one and discovered that the single glittery platform shoe was gone. And so was the braid of her hair.

Felix came up to stand behind her. "Whoa," he said when he saw the box's contents strewn about. "What's that, last year's Halloween costume? What did you go as? A drag queen, a swinger, or a hooker?"

She snapped her head around to glare at him. That last word just hit too hard in a place where she didn't need to be hit.

"I don't remember what I was for Halloween last year," she snapped. "I have amnesia. Remember?"

He immediately realized his gaffe. "I'm sorry, Rory. It was a joke. Those are just some pretty wild clothes. Whose are they?"

She sighed restlessly. She might as well just tell him. It wasn't like his opinion of her mattered.

He'd made clear he wanted nothing to do with her on any level other than helping her regain her memory, so what did she care if he drew the same conclusion about the outfit that she had herself?

But she realized she did care. As much as she'd promised herself there was no way she would get involved with Felix, as many times as she'd assured herself he wasn't the kind of guy she needed in her life, as certain as she'd been that she couldn't possibly have feelings for anyone because she didn't even know who she was... In spite of all of that, she definitely had feelings for Felix. Feelings she wasn't sure she even understood. Feelings she for sure shouldn't be having. Not until she solved the mystery of her identity and the particulars of her past. Not until she knew she could afford to get involved with someone.

Not that it mattered, she told herself again. Felix wanted nothing to do with her in that way. And even if he did, he wasn't going to be around much longer.

She met his gaze evenly and said, as levelly as she could, "They're my clothes. This is what the hospital returned to me when I was released. It's what I was wearing the night they found me tossed into the gutter in Gary."

His gaze changed from one of vague amusement to one of what she could only liken to shock.

"Yeah, I know," she said crisply. "The same thought occurred to me, too."

"What thought?" he asked with almost convincing bewilderment.

"That the only kind of woman who would wear stuff like this is a…is a…is…"

"Really bold and confident in her fashion choices?" he finished for her.

She tried to smile in response, but couldn't quite manage it. "That wasn't what I was thinking, no," she said. "I was thinking that, um, that maybe I haven't always made my living as a florist."

Now he was the one to meet her gaze levelly. "You said it was New Year's Eve the night you… had your accident."

"Yes."

He nodded toward the clothing. "You don't think plenty of people dress in flashy clothes on New Year's Eve?"

"Not when the temperature is in the single digits," she told him. It was like four degrees that night."

"Even so."

She looked at the clothes again. She just couldn't imagine any woman who wasn't up to something hinky wearing such clothes, especially on a bitterly cold night. And she certainly couldn't imagine the woman she knew herself to be at this point wearing something like that. Not unless she was doing it to make a living.

"I don't know…" she said, her voice trailing off. "I just can't see me wearing anything like this. I feel like the only reason I would have been was because I was…you know."

He threw her a halfhearted smile. "I don't think you were…you know."

"But what if I was, Felix?"

"Okay, what if you were?" he replied. "It's not that big a deal."

"It's a huge deal," she countered. "I don't want to be the kind of person who makes a living like that."

"You're borrowing trouble," he told her. "You have no idea what kind of person you were before you lost your memory, and even if you were a…you know…that doesn't make you any less of a person than anyone else."

She knew that. She did. People had to make a living however they could, and doing…you know…for money didn't make a person bad or immoral or anything else. There were plenty of so-called legitimate jobs that were anything but noble or ethical. Lobbyist, for example. Arms dealer. Paparazzo. Billionaire CEO. Jeez, you could say some of those were pretty much…you know…when it came to making money.

But Rory, at least the Rory she was now, didn't like the idea of doing that for a living. The Rory she was now wanted sex between two people to be a tender, emotional exchange borne of affection, not a simple physical one borne of commerce. She wanted to know the person she was with and care about them. She wanted it to be special.

And when had she decided all this? she wondered. She'd scarcely given sex a thought since waking up in the hospital eight months ago. She hadn't been attracted to anyone, hadn't had any desire to be with anyone, hadn't so much as fantasized about it. The fact that she had no idea who she was had always been a brutal reminder that she couldn't afford to get involved with anyone until she figured that out.

She looked at Felix again. Okay, that wasn't quite true. Over the past few days, being with him, she'd felt a twinge or two—or ten or twenty—of desire for him. And not just twinges. Wants. Yearnings. Needs. He just smelled so good all the time, whether it was thanks to his kitchen or his grooming. And he'd been so kind and patient in helping her regain her memory. And he had a way of smiling sometimes that made something in her stomach twitch and turn and spiral nearly out of control. Not to mention he was, you know, *sexy as hell.*

She remembered the afternoon in his grandmother's bedroom, when the two of them had been seated so close and speaking so low. She'd thought for a single, bewildering moment that he was going to kiss her. And in that moment, she'd wanted him to. Desperately. Almost like she wanted him to right now.

Instead, she gathered up the gaudy clothes and tucked them back into the box. She wondered if she should tell Felix about the missing shoe and braid. Whoever her intruder was, it looked like those were the only things they took. Why? Why take a single shoe and braid of hair and nothing else?

"It had to be Tracksuit Guy," she said.

Felix nodded. "Yeah, that's my thinking, too. He must have seen us drive off for the park and realized you wouldn't be home for a while. Me neither, for that matter. So he could make all the noise he wanted without anyone hearing him in here."

"But why would he go to all the trouble to break in and not take anything?" *Except for a single tacky shoe and a braid of hair?* she added to herself.

"Who knows?" Felix said. "Maybe he just wanted a more up close and personal view of you and your life."

"As if I needed anything else to make me feel super creeped out right now," she said. "I'm honestly feeling sick at the thought that he was here, touching my stuff, trying to find things out about me that he has no business knowing without my permission. I'm not going to sleep a wink tonight."

"You should stay at my place," Felix immediately offered.

Oh, right. Like that was going to help her sleep, being so close to him when she was feeling such a weird mix of raw emotion.

"Thanks, but that's okay," she told him. "I'll be fine."

"No, I'm serious, Rory. The lock is broken on both your doors. He didn't exactly finesse himself inside. He used a drill. You're going to have to call a locksmith tomorrow to replace them."

She closed her eyes. "Meaning he could get in again, even if I put in new locks. This whole thing just keeps getting better and better."

"Look, don't worry about it until tomorrow. Just stay at my place tonight. I have an extra room, after all."

She expelled a resigned sigh. He was right. No

way was if safe for her here tonight. Then again, was staying under the same roof as Felix going to be any better? There were a lot of different kinds of safety. And right now, there was one of them she wanted to throw right out the window.

"Thanks," she told him, pushing the thought away. "Just let me grab a few things."

"No problem," he replied. "I'll meet you out in the living room."

No problem, she echoed to herself. Yeah, right. There wasn't one problem. There were dozens. And, at this point, regaining her memory wasn't even at the top of the list anymore.

Chapter Ten

Normally, Felix didn't wake up until after nine, since he never had to be at work, really, before eleven—though he did tend to make his way down to the kitchen by ten, at the latest. He knew Rory started her day hours before his, though, so he set his alarm for six, got up, made coffee and prepped for breakfast, then took his time reading the news and watching Nestor survey the happenings on Water Street below.

Not that much seemed to be happening on Water Street at the moment. He was never awake this early and marveled at how quiet the neighborhood was at this hour. He heard the scrape of a manhole cover opening in the street below and the low murmurs of a couple of municipal workers. Once or twice, a car rattled by. And a noisy bird seemed to have lost his way and was cheep-cheep-cheeping to see if any of his friends answered. But other than that, everything was still.

It had never occurred to him that a quiet Endicott was a mellow Endicott. He'd always equated the lack of activity to lifelessness and tedium. His own life consisted almost entirely of the chaos and cacophony of his kitchen, and at night, he went to bed as soon as he got home so rarely noticed anything but the lack of activity outside. Even those few times when he got away from work, his hours were filled with the noises of his friends—their voices and laughter, the roar of the motor on Chance's runabout or the crash of the pins at Max's father's bowling alley or a million other things the three men did when they had time to get together that were always raucous and boisterous and fun.

Felix had just never noticed that the *quiet* of his hometown was also its peace. And he was surprised to realize he kind of liked it. Maybe he should get up early more often.

"Good morning."

He turned at the sound of Rory's voice and saw her standing in the living room entry. Nestor jumped down from his perch in the window to trot over and twine around and around her legs. She was wearing pajama pants decorated with cartoon breakfast foods and a T-shirt featuring one of the Powerpuff Girls—Bubbles, who happened to be his favorite, too. Her short hair was sticking up in tufts on her head, and she was rubbing her eyes as if she hadn't quite awoken. Coupled with the quiet outside and the dim light making its way through the windows, he was struck again by the alienness of his situation. It felt downright domestic in here. And wow, did that feel…nice? Never in a million years would Felix have thought domestic feelings were nice feelings. But damned if he didn't feel pretty good at the moment.

"You're up early," she said quietly. "I didn't think you had to be at work until ten or eleven."

It surprised him how much he liked the fact that she'd noticed what time he usually went to work. "I don't normally," he told her. "But I figured you'd need breakfast before you went in. And I know you go in a lot earlier than me."

So he'd noticed her comings and goings, too. So sue him.

She stopped rubbing her eyes and met his gaze. "That's nice of you, but I usually just have coffee, then grab a pastry or something at Bonita's midmorning."

Okay, so he didn't like so much that she went to Bonita's Bakery for her break instead of La Mariposa. They could work on that. He'd think later about why he thought working on that—or anything—with Rory was a good idea. Or why he was thinking about the two of them in terms of the future.

He made a playfully disappointed sound. "Breakfast is the most important meal of the day. And it should be mostly protein, not carbs."

She smiled and saluted him. "Thank you, Dr. Suarez, registered dietician."

"Oh, come on. Like you're going to turn down *huevos habaneros* and *café con leche*."

"How can I turn down *huevos habaneros* when I don't even know what they are? Though I recall that I have, in fact, had *café con leche*. And it is *muy delicioso,*" she added, smiling.

Smiling in a way that told him she wasn't surprised by the memory, as she had been so often in the past.

"You sound very matter-of-fact about that last one," he said. "Have you been having more memories you haven't told me about? And by the way," he added, "you'll love *huevos habaneros*, too."

She nodded, though which comment of his she

was nodding at, he didn't know. He decided to believe it was for both.

Nestor had, by now, gone from twining around her legs to putting his paws on her thighs and meowing plaintively. Felix couldn't have been more surprised when she picked up the cat matter-of-factly and cradled him in her arms, only to have him snuggle against her as if he'd been doing it all his life. Rory, too, seemed completely at ease with the activity. Clearly, she was a cat person. Which was probably what Nestor had responded to in her.

"I have actually been having more memories," she told him. "Last night, as I was drifting off to sleep, Nestor jumped into bed with me and nestled into the curve of my leg. And without thinking, I said, 'Good night, Sage.'"

"So your cat's name is Sage."

"Yep. I'm certain of it. I hope she's okay."

She gave Nestor a hug, and the cat nuzzled the curve joining her neck to her jaw. Felix felt inordinately envious.

He pushed the feeling away. Kind of. "I'm sure when you disappeared, someone stepped in to take care of her the way I did with Nestor for my grandmother. Hopefully better than I have," he added, "since that little derp has never responded to me the way he does to you."

She gave him another hug and set him gently on the ground. Instead of running away, Nestor sat diligently at her feet, glaring at Felix again and just daring him to not be nice to his newest, bestest friend.

"He's not a derp," she said. "He's just misunderstood."

Felix couldn't help grinning at both of them. His day—hell, his whole life—was just starting to feel so surreal this morning.

"I'm sure someone is taking care of your cat, too," he tried to reassure her. "I mean, I think we've established you have family and friends out there. We just don't know where."

"Somewhere along I-95," she said wistfully. "Somewhere with diners. Somewhere, maybe, with a professional women's basketball team."

"You know, that's a good point," Felix said. He grabbed his phone from the end table and began to type. "Not so much the diner part, but let's see where along I-95 there are WNBA teams."

Rory joined him, looking over his shoulder at the results that came up on his screen. She was still warm from bed, and her heat enveloped him, along with her scent, something that reminded him of an herb garden after a rain.

And, dios mío, *Suarez, could you be any more maudlin?*

"Here we go," he said when a list appeared. "Along I-95, there are teams in Washington, DC, New York and Connecticut. If you want to include other East Coast teams, all we have is Atlanta. You want to push it, Indiana has one, but you're already sure you're not from here. So, hey, that could potentially narrow it down. All the other teams are pretty much on, or on the other side of, the Mississippi."

He looked at Rory. She was looking back at him hopefully.

"You could be on to something," she said. "Especially if we throw in diners, since they seem to be more of a Northeast thing."

"So New York or Connecticut?" he asked.

She thought for a moment. "I don't think that's it exactly, but that area feels really good for some reason."

"Anything else you've remembered that might fill in the gaps?"

"Anything else I've remembered has come at night, in my dreams. Almost always from when I was young, and almost always with other people in them. I just can't see their faces."

She described in detail for him one dream where she was listening to music in a bedroom and another where she was talking to a girl at school.

"Most of your memories have come from your childhood or adolescence," he said when she finished. "Except for Sage the cat."

She nodded. "And the painting. I noticed that, too. I can't help thinking that all the memories that have come to me so far are from times and things that made me happy. Maybe memories of my present, except for Sage and being able to paint, are all..."

Her voice drifted off, as if she didn't want to put out in the universe that her adult life hadn't been a happy one. Had maybe even been pretty terrible. Felix didn't push it.

"Well, at least we're narrowing it down," he said.

"Maybe," she conceded. "It's still not definite."

"No, but it's more than we had before."

We, he realized. He'd just said *we*. Not *you*. He'd just told Rory that they both had more than they'd had before. Not her alone. Since when did he consider this crusade part of his life, too?

He rose from the couch. "I'll get you some coffee. And I'll have breakfast ready in about fifteen minutes."

"Thanks," she told him. She opened her mouth to say something else, then seemed to think better of whatever it was.

Knowing he shouldn't, Felix decided to ask anyway. "What?"

She shook her head again. "Nothing," she said softly. "Just…thanks, Felix. For everything."

There was a strange finality to her tone. Which was weird, because they still had so much to learn about her. Even so, he told her, "You're welcome."

She tilted her head back toward the bedroom where she'd spent the night, which had an attached bath. "I'm going to take a shower before breakfast, if that's okay."

"Sure," he told her.

"Just gimme five minutes."

And then she was disappearing down the hallway, completely oblivious to the fact that Felix was standing flummoxed in his living room. Not because he was amazed that anyone could shower in five minutes—himself included. Not because he was having trouble keeping images of Rory actually *in* the shower at bay —he was for sure having trouble with that. Not even because of all the stuff they'd learned that morning that could lead to finally uncovering her identity.

But because the simple exchange about breakfast they'd just shared had felt like the most natural thing in the world. As if waking up and making breakfast for Rory while she showered at his place was something the two of them did every day. And at how incredibly right—how incredibly *good*—that felt.

He scrubbed a hand through his hair and made himself think about Megan, and how abruptly she'd left his life—and him—and how devastated he'd been as a result of both. Strangely, though, he realized Megan was falling further and further back into the recesses of his brain, to be replaced by images of Rory instead.

Rory. Who could still leave him once she found out exactly who and what she really was.

It had been a surprisingly busy Thursday for Wallflowers, and Rory and Ezra were just starting to tidy up the back room when the high school senior who worked part-time in the shop came back to summon her. Hanh was wearing her usual goth makeup and black separates, right down to the heavily buckled motorcycle boots, even though the temperature outside today was pushing eighty. As she did every day, she had made herself a spiky boutonniere to complement the outfit—this one fashioned from eryngium and thistle—that looked super edgy and cool. Rory hoped Hanh never quit her job here.

"There's a guy out front who wants to talk to you," she told Rory, jutting a black-tipped thumb over her shoulder toward the front of the store.

"Who is it?" Rory asked.

"Dunno," Hanh told her with a shrug. "He didn't give me a name, and I didn't ask."

Oh, to be as carefree as a teenager in Endicott, Indiana, Rory thought. To never have to be suspicious of anyone. To assume no one had nefarious plans. To know your real name and where you came from and never have to question that someone out there in the world might know more about you than you knew yourself, so you never had to be on your guard and never had to just hope like hell everyone you met only had good intentions.

"Not a customer, though," Hanh added.

"How do you know?"

"He didn't even look around when he came into the shop. He just looked straight at me and said he needed to talk to my boss."

Rory couldn't imagine anyone doing that. Her neighbors would have come in the back way to talk to her or say hello, the way all of them did who owned shops on Water Street. And, honestly, she didn't really know anyone else in town. She'd done her best to keep to herself. Besides, none of them ever referred to each other as a *boss*. That was way too Gen X.

"Tell him I'll be right out," Rory said.

Hanh spun on her heel to return to the shop.

"Problem?" Ezra asked when he noticed her apprehension.

"I don't think so," Rory told him. "I just can't imagine who would be asking for me if they're not a customer."

"Maybe it's someone who ordered something online," he suggested. "Maybe we screwed it up or didn't give them what they wanted."

That was probably it. Surprisingly, the fact that Rory might have hacked off a customer by messing up was a far more appealing prospect than anything she could imagine otherwise. She brightened.

Ezra chuckled when he noted her happier demeanor. "It is so weird, the things that make you happy."

Rory laughed, too. "No, it's not that I'm happy I might have alienated a customer. It's that—"

She stopped herself. No one in Endicott besides Felix knew about Rory's amnesia. She'd learned well how to fake her way through life in the months before she arrived here. Ezra was probably her closest friend besides Felix, and she never saw him outside of work. He suspected nothing. No way was she going to try to explain her condition to him. Not yet, anyway.

"Never mind," she told him with a smile. "I'll be right back."

Her smile fell, however, the moment she entered her shop. Because Tracksuit Guy was standing in the middle of it, today wearing his dress-up outfit of burgundy with red stripes, which she now saw was velour—a surprising choice, considering both the current meteorological and fashion climates. He had his hands on his hips, his jaw thrust upward, his lips pursed and his eyebrows lowered. She'd never seen him this close-up before, and she was surprised to realize he was younger than she'd thought—he didn't look much older than Hanh. His dark hair was long but shoved straight back from his face, his dark eyes were fringed by thick lashes, and a scar bisected one sable brow.

He actually wasn't bad looking for a kid, she couldn't help thinking. Hanh seemed to think so, too, because she kept sneaking peeks at him from behind the counter. There was no mistaking the aggression in his pose, though, and Rory couldn't imagine what he had to feel aggressive about. *He* was the one who had broken into *her* place—she was sure of it. She should be the one in attack mode. Instead, she wanted very badly to turn tail and run. Even so, his young age made her feel less frightened of him than she might have otherwise. Even so, she still wasn't keen to have him in her shop.

"I'm Rory Vincent," she said as calmly as she could, even though she was reasonably certain he already knew that. "Can I help you?"

"Yeah," he said. "I'm lookin' for somethin' nice for my, um, my aunt. My great-aunt. Aunt Donatella. Yeah, that's it."

There was a huge dose of the Northeast in his accent—Rory had streamed enough TV by now to recognize the cadences of North Jersey and Long Island, New York. This guy sounded like a stereotype straight out of *The Sopranos*.

"Well, I'm sure Hanh here will be happy to help you put something together," Rory told him. "She's got a great eye. Or we have a catalogue of prearranged selections that are popular with our customers. You can flip through it to see if you like something in there. Hanh can answer any questions you might have."

Tracksuit Guy dropped his hands from his hips and took a few steps forward. Without thinking, Rory took a few steps in retreat. When he noted her withdrawal, he stopped and eyed her warily.

"I like workin' with the boss of a place," the guy said. "It's how I do business, you know?"

Actually, Rory didn't, but okay. She wasn't one to think the customer was always right—since they often weren't—but fine. The sooner she got Tracksuit Guy out of her store, the better. If that meant dealing with him herself, she'd put something together as quickly as she could and then hustle him out of her shop.

"Okay then," she said. "What's the occasion?"

Tracksuit Guy had to think about that for a second, then blurted out, "First Communion."

"Your great-aunt is just now making her First Communion?" she asked.

He looked a little flummoxed by the question. "*Uuuhhh…*yeah. Yeah. She converted. To marry my uncle Basilio."

"I see," Rory said. "So she's kind of a newlywed, as well?"

At this, Tracksuit Guy shrugged. "Sure. Why not?"

Rory nodded. "Well, I've never done an arrangement for a combination occasion like First Communion and bridal, so this will be a learning experience for both of us."

"Va bene."

All right, Rory translated easily. "So…does your aunt Donatella have a favorite flower, Mr.…?" Rory asked, shamelessly fishing for a name.

"Frankie," he told her. "Frankie is good."

There was no way she was going to be able to call him Frankie with a straight face. Calling someone who talked and looked like him *Frankie* would just distract her, making her wonder if he had a cool mafia nickname like they did in the movies. Frankie "Fettuccini" Ferrari or something.

"Okay, Mr. Fettu… Uh…okay, Frankie," she said. Yeah, no. She was just going to have to sidestep the whole name thing. "Does Aunt Donatella have a favorite flower?"

He shrugged again, then looked around the room. His gaze finally lit on a bucket full of gerbera daisies. "Those look okay, I guess," he said.

"Great choice," Rory told him, even though she probably would have chosen something else for a combo First Communion/wedding. Something bizarre and inappropriate and actually kinda gross to fit such an occasion. She just wanted to get Frankie "Fettuccini" Ferrari out of her store ASAP.

She spent the next fifteen minutes putting together an arrangement for him that ended up being surprisingly coherent, considering the way her brain was scrambling for thoughts the entire time. She'd expected him to spend the time asking her a lot of invasive questions about herself, but he'd only acted as if he were sincerely concerned about whether or not his probably fictional aunt Donatella would like her bouquet. Then he paid—in cash, naturally—and exited Wallflowers with his purchase, turning left to make his way down Water Street.

Before the door swung closed behind him, though, she heard him start whistling "Fly Me to the Moon" again, and a chill actually went down her spine.

"He was cute," Hanh said. "Kind of a weirdo. But cute."

Definitely a weirdo, Rory thought. And, to her, at least, in no way cute.

"Hanh, if he comes in again, let me know, okay?"

Hanh looked at her, clearly concerned. "You think he's dangerous?"

"Maybe."

Now Hanh smiled. "Cool."

Rory shook her head. Maybe it wasn't so great to be a teenager in Endicott, Indiana. No sense of self-preservation whatsoever. Even though it was still half an hour to closing time, she crossed to the front door and locked it.

"Go ahead and close the register," she told Hanh. "I think we're done for the day."

Chapter Eleven

"*Chica*, I just had the weirdest day at the restaurant that I've ever had in my life."

Felix looked at Rory, who was standing on the other side of her front door—next to, he couldn't help noticing, her newly installed keypad lock—in pajama pants spattered with red rosebuds and a red T-shirt...and who was staring back at him with much annoyance. Okay, so maybe coming to her place unannounced after midnight wasn't something he normally did. Or, you know, ever did. At least not before this week. It had just been that kind of day. All day. From the minute Rory had walked sleepily into his living room looking like she belonged there, all the way up to dinner. Dinner had actually been the strangest part of all.

"Felix, I was just about to turn in," she told him. "I had a pretty weird day, too."

"Oh, no," he told her. "Not until I tell you who came into La Mariposa tonight."

"Tracksuit Guy," she replied without missing a beat.

His eyebrows shot up at that. "Yeah. How did you know?"

"He came into my shop, too."

His eyebrows couldn't go any higher, so his mouth dropped open instead. "And you were going to tell me about this when?"

"Tomorrow," she said. "La Mariposa was just getting into the swing by the time it happened. I was going to tell you tonight, but I stopped outside the kitchen door before coming in because you were yelling something in Spanish that sounded like you were in deep doo-doo. I didn't want to interrupt you."

Felix tried to remember the moment she described, then figured it could have been just about any moment that evening. So he only said, "You could've interrupted me to tell me that."

She shook her head wearily. "All he did was buy an arrangement for someone who probably doesn't even exist. Hanh was in the shop with me the whole time. And Ezra was in back. Frankie didn't—"

"Frankie?" Felix interjected. "He actually gave you a name?"

"Only a first name. And that probably wasn't real, either. He paid in cash, so…"

"You should've told me," Felix repeated.

"It was fine, Felix. I was going to tell you all about it tomorrow."

"Well, after he came in to see you, he stopped in to see me. And *dios mío, que bicho raro*."

"Sorry," Rory said, "but that's beyond my translation ability."

"What a weirdo," Felix told her.

"Did the weirdo at least pay with a credit card?" Rory asked hopefully. "With his full name on it? That we could google and find out where he lives?"

"No," Felix told her. "He paid in cash. But I mean, come on. That accent? He had to be from New York or New Jersey."

"No kidding."

When she didn't seem to make the connection he had, Felix added, "You know. Probably somewhere around I-95."

Her eyes snapped open at that. "Oh, wow. I was so exhausted by the time I had to deal with him, that never even occurred to me." She opened her door wider. "You should probably come in."

He shook his head. "No, you should come out."

She looked at him with even more annoyance than before. "Felix, you may have noticed I'm kind of in for the night."

"That's okay. I was going to invite you to do this anyway tonight, but now that we have a lot to talk about, it's even more important."

"Do what? What's so important?"

"Just come out."

She looked like she was going to balk. Then, softly, she said, "Let me just grab a jacket."

It was the first time he'd noticed how much cooler the night was than the day that had preceded it. Although he'd gone home after work long enough to shower and change into a white T-shirt and black sweatpants, he still felt hot from the kitchen as he always did, even hours after knocking off for the day. Rory returned, having thrown on a white hoodie, and started to make her way to the other door that led to the stairs outside. But Felix stopped her.

"We're not going out that way," he said.

She looked confused.

He tilted his head to the right. "We're going out that way."

His statement only compounded her confusion. "But the only thing down there is the roof access."

He smiled. "Don't tell me that in the whole time you've lived here, you've never gone up to the roof."

"Only when I looked at the place before buying it."

He shook his head in disappointment. The roof was one of his favorite places to go. Some of his first memories of his childhood had been when Tita had taken him up there with her to watch the fireworks for the Fourth of July and New Year's Eve. She'd make them a big bowl of popcorn and a pitcher of Kool-Aid—he'd had simple tastes when he was a toddler—and they'd unfold a blanket and throw down some pillows, and he would stay up way past his bedtime and feel like the luckiest kid in the world. The rooftop was a magical place, saved only for the most momentous occasions. And tonight was certainly one of those.

She shrugged. "I've never had any other reason to go up to there."

Felix grinned. "Well, tonight, you do."

She sighed heavily. "Fine."

"Bueno."

He extended his hand to the right, as if he were a circus ringmaster leading her to the most magical event of the evening. Which he kind of was, but let her figure that out for herself. She locked her door behind herself—couldn't be too careful after having her place broken into—then made her way past Felix and the door to her storeroom to the ladder at the end of the hall. Hanging at shoulder height was a key, and she plucked it from the hook before placing her foot on the first rung.

At the top of the ladder was a metal hatch with a padlock that she made short work of. Then she pushed it upward with a rusty *creeeaaak*. He had the same setup in his own place, but he never bothered to lock his hatch. Until now, he'd wondered why anyone would bother. But after what happened to Rory last night, he was starting to reconsider.

Nah, he told himself. Her break-in hadn't been some random act of mischief and mayhem. It had been the result of someone who'd targeted her specifically because he was specifically interested in her. Which actually made it worse. But if Frankie the tracksuit guy had wanted to hurt Rory, he'd had plenty of opportunity to do that. It looked like, until last night, anyway, he'd just wanted to snoop around in the shadows.

So why had he made himself so blatantly known—to both of them—today?

Once Rory was safely up top, Felix swiftly followed. When he exited the hatch onto her roof, he found her standing in the middle of it, her arms at her sides, staring up at the sky. The sky that was spattered with what looked like billions of stars, interrupted by a thin slice of moon and a comet winking to its left. Bob was a little brighter tonight than he was last night. In a couple of hours, he'd be making his pass as close to the planet as he would be this year. But he'd be visible to the naked eye for another week or so before disappearing onto his next journey around the sun.

All over town tonight, teenagers who'd been born in Endicott the last time Bob came around would be making wishes for things they wanted to have or happen fifteen years from now. The same way he had himself when he was that age. Felix couldn't imagine where he would be fifteen years from tonight. But looking at Rory right now…

"I can't believe we can still see so many stars," she said, "even being in the heart of town, with the streetlights on."

"Yeah, well, part of Old Town Endicott's charm is the old-fashioned streetlights that only give off about as much light as the gas ones they were a couple centuries ago," he said. Not to mention that the trees planted around the same time obscured much of the illumination over them this high up. "So, yeah. Pretty easy to see the night sky up here. But we're not going to watch it from your roof," he added.

She turned to look at him, curious.

He dipped his head to the right again. "We're going next door to my place."

A short brick wall separated each of the storefront properties along the building, low enough for them to lever themselves over it. Felix was kind of surprised when Rory followed him without question, but she did. Once they crossed to his side, he held up both arms to create an L-shape, once again the ringmaster, to frame the scene he'd set out before going to her place—a blanket on the ground with two pillows on one side and a pair of Collins glasses on the other. Beside them was a frosty ice bucket filled with ice, along with a cocktail shaker full of mojitos. The perfect comet-watching setup.

She chuckled softly when she saw it. "What's all this?"

"Comet Bob is at his closest point to the planet tonight," Felix told her. "It's kind of a special night around here. Fifteen-year-olds all over town are wishing harder tonight than they did on Christmas Eve when they still believed in Santa."

Rory continued to smile as she drew nearer. "Yeah, well, Santa ended up not being real, didn't t he? But a comet that you can actually see in the sky? That's gotta be a sure thing, right?"

He remembered telling her what he wished for when he was fifteen. For something *interesting* to happen in Endicott. He looked at Rory again. When she'd first told him about her amnesia, he'd thought the whole thing was ridiculous, not interesting. Since then, however… Well, now Felix couldn't help thinking that Bob had definitely delivered for him.

He sat on the blanket and reached for the cocktail shaker, giving it a couple of swirls before pouring the first of two glasses. "Hey, Rory," he said.

She turned, and, when she saw him sitting on the blanket, covered the half-dozen strides it took to join him. "What?" she asked on the way.

"If you were a fifteen-year-old kid this year," he said, "and you could make a wish on the comet that would come true when you were thirty, what would you wish for? And I know," he added as she sat down beside him, her mouth open to object, "you don't remember who or where you were when you were fifteen." He handed her the mojito, then went to pour one for himself. "But pretend. Think about the girl with the pink bedroom who wanted a horse for her birthday and to play for the WNBA. And who rode in the back of a big car while her dad sang Frank Sinatra tunes to her. And who danced barefoot at her friend's quinceañera to 'Gasolina.' What would she have wished for?"

She looked at him in clear astonishment, but said nothing.

"What?" he asked.

She shook her head in wonder. "Wow, you really were listening to me."

He found the remark odd. "Of course I was listening. Why wouldn't I be?"

She smiled again, but there was something a little melancholy in the gesture this time. "I don't know. But for some reason, I feel surprised that someone was actually paying attention to me."

The comment hit Felix harder than it probably should have. Just what kind of life had Rory been living when she lost her memory? He pushed the thought away and continued, "Anyway, think about her. What do you think she would have wished for?"

Rory inhaled a deep breath and held it, then closed her eyes and turned her face up to the night sky. "I think..." she began. "I think she would have wished for..."

A long minute passed, one he knew better than to interrupt. Finally, she nodded once, then opened her eyes and gazed at the sky again, right where Bob was flashing back at her. And he knew then what she had done.

"What did you wish for?" he asked.

Now she turned to look at Felix. "I wished that Bob would let her grow up to be herself. Whoever that ended up being."

At first, Felix thought it was kind of an odd wish. But after a moment, he thought he understood.

"You think you were unhappy, the way you were living before your accident, because you were living for someone else instead of yourself," he said. It was a statement, not a question, because it was suddenly pretty obvious.

She nodded. "Yeah, I do. I think I was unhappy, at any rate. There have been so many times this week when there have been visions and impressions, just out of my reach, that I know were twinges of recent memory. But as soon as I thought I knew what they were, as soon as I thought they were going to materialize into something concrete and tell me who I really am *now* and where I really live *now and* what I'm really doing *now*, they evaporated again without telling me any more than that maybe I'm just happier not knowing those things."

He shrugged. "Maybe you are."

"Maybe..." She took a sip of her drink. "Hey, this is really good."

"Better than a dirty martini, right?"

She enjoyed another taste. "Yeah. Way better. Thanks."

"You're welcome."

Rory smiled at him. Felix smiled back. A feeling settled over them that wasn't exactly awkward, but wasn't quite comfortable, either. For a long moment, they only sipped their drinks and gazed at each other, and he tried really hard to think of something to say. For some reason, though, talking didn't quite feel necessary.

Rory finally broke the silence with "So, my life before the accident."

Right. They were supposed to be talking about real things, not getting lost in something nebulous he couldn't even identify.

She continued, "Do you think Frankie is part of the life I left behind?"

Felix nodded. "I do, actually. In some way."

"Then why didn't he tell me that?"

"I don't know. But he's definitely got some link to you."

"But is it my Spanish-speaking me or my Italian-speaking me?"

"Definitely Italian," Felix said. "Marita served him at La Mariposa tonight, and she said he barely looked at the menu, that when he saw spaghetti—which is actually chicken spaghetti that's just on the kids' menu, because they can be so picky—

he immediately ordered it. I mean, adults order it sometimes, if they don't think they're going to like Cuban food, and that's cool. But why come into a Cuban restaurant in the first place if you don't like Cuban food? And this guy… *Dios mío*."

"What happened?" Rory asked.

"Marita said she put it on the table and he dug right in, then spit it out again. Actually spit it out," Felix repeated indignantly, feeling outraged all over again. "Then he demanded she get him the menu, and he reread the description. Then he got mad all over again and demanded to see me. And when I went to the table, before I could even say a word, he lit into me, asking me what the hell are sazon and adobo, and what in the name of God are they doing in spaghetti sauce, which should have basil and oregano, and oh, by the way, there's a typo on the menu, since it should be pollo *di*, spaghetti not pollo *de*—duh—and what the hell did I think I was doing using chicken in spaghetti in the first place, that was just an affront to God and pasta both."

He could see Rory trying to hide a smile, but not very well.

"It's not funny," Felix said.

She bit her lip to keep her smile from growing bigger. "Of course it isn't."

"It's *not*. I take a lot of pride in my menu. That guy had no idea what he was talking about."

"Clearly," Rory agreed. Still smiling. "But that does make him sound pretty Italian, all right. Also, the almost certainly phony aunt he was buying flowers for was named Donatella, and she had allegedly just married his uncle Basilio, so… Yeah. Definitely part of my Italian life."

"Yeah, if he'd been Latino, he would have loved that spaghetti."

Rory sighed. "I should tell you something else."

His stomach knotted at the sound of apprehension in her voice. "What?"

"The night he broke into my apartment?"

"Yeah?"

"He did steal something. Actually, two things."

Her admission surprised Felix. He would have thought that by now, the two of them could have told each other anything. Then he asked himself why he would assume that, when he'd never given Rory any reason to feel that way. Over the past few days, he'd spent way too much time assuring her he was only with her because she was pressuring him to be with her and had made clear, right off the bat, that he wanted nothing to do with helping her figure out who she was. Then he made clear that the only reason he was with her was to help her figure out who she was, and that was it.

How could he have told her that? he wondered now. How could he have wanted to keep her at arm's length? Especially when, at the moment, all he wanted to do was pull her into his arms and hold her close.

"What did he steal?" he asked instead.

"A shoe," she told him.

"A shoe?" he echoed. "As in *one* shoe?"

She nodded. "This really tacky, glittery shoe I was wearing with all the really tacky clothes I had on the night of my accident."

"Why would he take one shoe?"

"Because I only had one shoe."

"Why did you only have one shoe?"

"Because the other one got lost somewhere that night. I was only wearing one shoe when the paramedics found me."

"So…what?" Felix asked. "He's going to do some kind of reverse Cinderella thing and try to match that shoe to the one you lost?"

She shook her head. "I don't know."

Felix studied her in silence for a moment. Every time he thought Rory's situation couldn't get any weirder, it got weirder.

"You said he took two things," he continued.

Now she nodded. "He took a braid of my hair."

And there it went again, getting weirder still. Had Felix been confused before? 'Cause now, his head was starting to spin. "He took what?"

"I had really long hair when I had my accident," she told him. "But they had to shave a section of it off to treat my head injury. Obviously, it looked terrible, missing a chunk like that, so, when I got out of the hospital, I went to a salon and had the rest of my hair cut short enough to even it up as much as possible. The stylist braided what she chopped off and gave it back to me. I honestly don't know why I kept it. I guess I just figured I'd lost so much of myself at that point, I wanted to hang on to whatever I could, so I stuck it in the box with everything else. But here's the thing, Felix."

There was only one thing? 'Cause he could think of way more than that. "What?" he said.

"My hair was *really* long. Nearly to my waist. And it was dyed blond and highlighted—not dark, like it is now. I can't imagine having hair that long or coloring it the way it was. I mean, I want to grow it out more, but not to my waist. And I like my natural color. Why would I have such long, flashy hair when it's so not me?"

"And why would some weirdo steal it?" he said.

"That, too. It's just so bizarre. Between him

taking my shoe and then coming into the shop today—and La Mariposa, too—it makes me think he knows more about me than I do. Like maybe he was just getting closer today to confirm a suspicion he already had after breaking into my apartment."

"Like maybe he knows who you are," Felix said, filling in what she was clearly skirting around.

"Yeah," she said. "Like that."

"But then why didn't he say something?" Felix asked.

She shook her head again. "I wish I knew. But at least now, we can maybe know for sure that I'm from New York or New Jersey. Which begs the question, what was I doing in Gary, Indiana?"

"Or Chicago," Felix pointed out. "They're right next to each other. You could have been visiting someone in Chicago. Or maybe you moved there."

She made a restless sound, took another sip of her drink, then set the glass on the ground. Then she lay back on the blanket with her head on one pillow, and her arm under that, and stared up at the sky.

"Can we talk about something else?" she asked.

Felix lay down on the blanket beside her, on his side, his head propped in his hand. "Hell, yes," he told her. "Frankie—seriously, what grown man calls himself that?—isn't what I wanted to talk about anyway when I planned this tonight."

She looked up at him, smiling. It wasn't a heartfelt smile. She was clearly bothered by the exchange they'd just had. But it was still a smile. "Planned what tonight?" she asked. "Aren't we just going to comet watch?"

Well, that was what he'd thought when he made the plans. The way she was looking at him now, though…

"I figured you'd want to make a wish," he said, sidestepping the question. Which she had done, so what was on the agenda now?

"And I did," she told him. "Hopefully, it won't take fifteen years to come true."

Now Felix shifted to his back and stared at the sky, too. "Who says it hasn't already come true? Everything you've learned about your adult self is stuff you say you can't imagine being your life now, right?"

"Yes."

"And you wished the girl you were could grow up to be herself. Whoever that ended up being. So maybe, if nothing else, that's a gift your amnesia has given you. You've become yourself."

She turned her head to look at him. He turned his head to look at her, too.

"That's the first time you've said 'amnesia' out loud," she told him.

Was it? Then he thought about it. Yeah, it was. Every time the word had entered his head before, he'd pushed the idea away and phrased it as something else out loud. Because amnesia had been such an alien concept. Like something only crazy people would have. But Rory wasn't crazy. And she sure as hell wasn't alien. Not to him. Not anymore.

"Maybe I'm not as uncomfortable with it as I was before," he said. "Maybe I don't think it's crazy so much as it is—"

"What?" she asked.

He smiled. "Interesting. You're very interesting, Rory Vincent."

She grinned, and this time the sadness was gone. "So Bob granted both our wishes."

"I guess he did."

She moved her hand the few inches between them, and wove her fingers with his. As if it were the most natural thing in the world to do. And, weirdly, it did feel natural.

"Thanks, Felix," she said quietly.

He entwined his fingers with hers, weaving them together more snugly. "For what?"

She looked back up at the sky. "For helping me

out. For talking to me and letting me talk to you. For being my friend."

Was that what they were? Friends? 'Cause he'd sure never felt this way about any of his friends before. Not even Megan.

"And for just," she continued, "I don't know. For not thinking I'm a complete wacko."

"You're not a wacko."

She said nothing in response to that, only looked at him again. This time, when she smiled, it was…wistful. Maybe even hopeful. Like she didn't feel quite as lost as she had been a few days ago.

In the faint light of the moon and stars overhead—and hell, Bob, too—she looked almost otherworldly, as if she were a gift from the cosmos sent to earth to help Felix… What? Find his way? Figure stuff out? Make his life interesting for a change? Because somehow, she'd done all those things. And more. Rory wasn't the only one who was suddenly feeling less lost. Over the past few days, she'd made him start to understand what was really important in life. A sense of self. A sense of place. A sense of belonging. Even though he'd never had amnesia, he'd been feeling as adrift and muddled in his life as she did in hers. Since coming to know her, though, he felt as if he'd come to know himself, too.

Maybe the reason he was still in Endicott after all these years wasn't because he hadn't figured out his place beyond it. Maybe it was because he hadn't figured out his place here. Maybe, deep down, he didn't want to leave Endicott. Maybe he'd just needed to find his purpose here. He'd always thought his purpose was La Mariposa. Now, though, somehow, he was beginning to realize it was so much more.

Still holding her hand, he turned to his side again, looking at Rory. She still looked wistful. She still looked hopeful. She still looked more beautiful than anyone—anything—he'd ever seen. Without thinking about what he was doing—without even realizing he was doing it, even—he moved closer to her, pushing himself back up on his elbow. Then, slowly, he began to lower his head toward hers. When her eyes widened in realization of what he intended to do, he hesitated. But she lifted her free hand to cup it around his nape and softly urged him closer. And when he covered her mouth with his, she welcomed him with a warmth and desire that mirrored his own.

He had thought their first kiss would be more passionate—and when had he begun to think there would be a first kiss?—but, instead, it was as soft and gentle as the breeze skimming over them. They kissed as if they were getting to know each other, and, in a way, he supposed they were. They were getting to know each other up close instead of at a distance. They hadn't even touched each other before now, not really. Not unless he included the basketball game between them earlier, and that had been anything but affectionate. Now, though…

Now he wanted to be affectionate with Rory. He wanted to learn how she felt, how she sounded, how she moved, when the two of them were coming together. He wanted to know…everything. Everything there was to know about her. Whether or not she regained her memory wasn't important. What she'd been, where she'd been, who she'd been… None of that mattered. What was important was what she was now. What he was now. What they were now.

For long moments, they only kissed, getting accustomed to each other. As Rory threaded her fingers into Felix's hair, he moved his hand to her hip, pulling her closer to him. She turned on her side, too, to better fit her body to his, and he rolled onto his back to pull her atop him. She kissed him more deeply, and he wrapped both arms around her waist to pull her even closer, tasting her more passionately.

That was when Rory suddenly stilled. She

didn't withdraw from him, didn't release him, didn't push him away. She just…stopped. Stopped kissing him, stopped curling his hair around her fingers, stopped strumming his rib cage with an idle hand. Slowly, she pulled her head back and looked at him, her eyes filled with wonder. And, somehow, instinctively, Felix knew to not move a muscle or say a word.

For a long time, she only studied him in silence, her gaze never leaving his. And then, very softly, she told him, "I remember, Felix. I remember everything."

Chapter Twelve

At first, the memories crept back to Rory gradually, tiptoeing into her brain almost apologetically, as if returning home from a regrettable all-nighter. Then they started tumbling in a little faster, then faster still, until they were rushing so quickly, she was helpless to stop them. Her school years, her teen years, her twenties. She remembered a brightly colored house in Elizabeth, New Jersey, filled with knickknacks and fringe, remembered her nonna Bella caring for her because her mother died shortly after she was born. She remembered her father, Nardo, doting on her when she was a child, then their relationship growing rocky and distant as she grew into a young woman with a mind of her own, until he only spoke to her to let her know what a disappointment she was.

And she remembered her best friend since kindergarten, Carmen Montero, whose Puerto Rican parents owned the flower shop where Rory helped out as a little girl and got her first job when she was sixteen. It was the Montero family she'd been recalling whenever Felix spurred her memories. Because it was only when she was with the Monteros that Rory had been truly happy. They had loved her the way she was, even after her father's rejection of her—especially after her father's rejection of her—no questions asked, no judgments uttered, no conditions made.

At least until they moved to the other side of the country shortly after Rory and Carmen graduated from high school. After that, with no one else to make her feel loved—with no one else for her to love in return—Rory had begun to do whatever she could to win back her father's affections, even if it meant saying and being things she never would have said or done or been otherwise. She'd behaved the same way when it came to boys, because no boys she knew had ever wanted to date her the way she was. That was when she'd begun to dress and act like the other daughters in her father's social circle, and when she'd started to date boys of whom she knew her father would approve.

But it wasn't just her childhood and adolescence in Elizabeth that came rushing back to Rory. She also remembered everything that happened prior her accident. She remembered getting off a plane at O'Hare on Christmas Eve and waiting for her fiancé, Marco DiNunzio, at baggage check. Yes, her *fiancé*, because her father and Marco's had been childhood friends and had talked about the two of them marrying from the time they were in diapers. And waiting, and waiting, and waiting for him, until Marco finally showed up forty-five minutes after their agreed-upon time, telling her she was crazy, that he was there exactly when he'd told her he would be. She remembered staying at his place in the Loop for Christmas, but hardly ever seeing him because he was always so busy and rarely at home. She remembered them fighting—a lot. And she remembered New Year's Eve, when the two of them left his place in a hired car to go to meet friends, but not before he picked something up in Gary, he said.

And she remembered the "thing" he had to pick up in Gary was a girl named Angie who looked like she was barely out of high school. And he told Rory if she didn't like it, she could get out at the next corner.

Rory had been appalled and angry on so many levels, she hadn't known where to begin. She went after Marco with the fury of both a woman scorned and a mama bear. She actually got physical with him, she recalled, battering him with her giant handbag and kicking at his shins with her tacky platform shoes until one of them came off. At some point during the melee, he grabbed her bag and tossed it to the other side of the car, yelling for the driver to stop. But before the driver even had a chance, Marco opened the door and shoved her out of the car with all his might. She remembered a jagged pain piercing her head as the car went speeding off, just before she lost consciousness.

"What are you remembering, Rory?"

Felix's voice came to her as if from under water and a million miles away.

"All of it," she told him.

"Just like that?"

She nodded. "Just like that."

She moved away from him, but didn't go far, only lay on her back beside him, staring at the sky again. It really was beautiful, a dark backdrop mottled with stars that made her think of diamonds scattered across black velvet. She'd seen that very thing once, when she was in middle school, when she'd walked into her kitchen after school and seen her father standing by another man, the two of them inspecting the gems with jeweler's loupes. He'd told her to hurry up and fix herself a snack, then go to her room to do her homework. She remembered the event as if it had happened yesterday.

Felix turned to his side and propped himself on an elbow again, looking down at her with obvious concern, almost as if he were afraid to ask for details about all the things that were tumbling back into her brain. She didn't blame him. Most of the details of her life that she was recalling—at least the ones that didn't include Carmen and her family—weren't exactly pleasant.

Thankfully, he started with any easy one. "What's your real name?"

She smiled at that, because she'd been fairly close when she landed on a name for herself at the hospital. "Aurora," she told him. "My name is Aurora Venturi."

He chuckled softly at that. "Definitely Italian."

She smiled back. "Ya think?"

"Where are you from?"

"Elizabeth, New Jersey," she told him. "My father is Nardo Venturi, and he...he's a businessman, I think." Even with her memories coming back, she still wasn't sure she knew exactly what her father did for a living. But she hadn't really known that before losing her memory, either. He'd always seemed to have interests in a lot of different areas. "He owns stuff," she finally told Felix. "A construction company, a sanitation company, a night club, and an ice cream parlor."

Felix's brows arrowed down at that.

"What?" she asked.

"Nothing," he told her,

"You look worried suddenly."

"It's just..."

"What?"

He jackknifed up to sitting. Rory did the same.

He expelled a restless sound. "Just... New Jersey? Italian? Construction and sanitation companies and a night club?"

"Yeah. So?"

He eyed her warily. "So how many Martin Scorsese movies have you seen?"

It was an odd question to ask, but she replied, "None. Why?"

He studied her for another moment in silence, then his expression cleared. Mostly. "Never mind," he said. "So how do you know Spanish in addition to Italian?"

"My best friend all through school was a girl named Carmen Montero. Her parents moved to New Jersey from Puerto Rico and owned a flower shop. I spent as much time with them as I could. Mr. and Mrs. Montero were more parents to me than my own father was. First, because he was too busy with work to be around much, and then later, because—" She stopped before saying more.

"Later, because why?" Felix asked.

"Later, because I reached an age where I started to rebel. Typical teenage stuff. Nothing major." She met his gaze levelly. "But he didn't like it when I went from being a little girl who idolized him to being a bigger girl who didn't quite fit the mold he wanted to keep her in."

"And what kind of girl was that?"

"A girl with a mind of her own. A mind that held a lot of ideas and opinions he didn't hold himself."

She could tell Felix understood immediately. "Like thinking you should dress like a nice girl and follow his rules instead of putting on a school basketball uniform for an aggressive full-court press."

She nodded. "Yeah. Like that."

"What about your mother?" he asked.

"She died when I was a baby. I never knew her. Her mother, my nonna Bella, helped raise me until she died. When I was twelve."

Rory told Felix everything of significance from her life, spilling every detail that was pertinent, right up to the night when she and Marco had their big blowup and how that ended.

"This guy was your *fiancé*?" Felix asked incredulously.

"Only because my father and his father wanted to see us married, and at that point, I was doing whatever I could to please my father. And Marco, for that matter. I didn't love him. He obviously didn't love me. I mean, he must have seen my photo on the news when the police were trying to find someone to identify me, because they circulated it all over Chicago, on TV and in the newspapers. But he didn't even come forward to identify me, and he obviously didn't let anyone else I'd met come forward, either. He just let me stay a Jane Doe."

Felix said, "Probably because if your father found out what Marco did, he would have him whacked."

It was the second odd statement he'd made about her father. "What do you mean?"

He only shook his head and repeated, "Nothing. Never mind. You should press charges against him for assault."

"I will. That bastard won't get away with what he did. I can't wait to see his face when he finds out I remember everything. He's arrogant enough to think I'll just keep toeing the line and fuhgeddaboudit."

She slapped a hand over her mouth at that. Felix's eyebrows shot up.

"Did you hear that?" she asked from around her fingers.

"The 'Fuhgeddaboudit?'" he parroted. "Yeah."

"I'm talkin' like I'm from New Jersey," she said. Talking like she was from New Jersey.

"You are from New Jersey," he reminded her.

"Yeh, but—" She slapped her hand over her mouth again. "I did it again," she said. "I said 'yeh,' not 'yeah.'"

Felix eyed her with much interest. "Is it possible that, with your amnesia, you forgot to talk with your accent?"

"I dunno. I'll hafta google it." But there was no mistaking it now. She was definitely a Jersey girl. "Oh. My. Gawd."

Felix chuckled a little at that, but he looked as confused as she was. She didn't feel like Aurora Venturi, Jersey girl. But she didn't quite feel like Rory Vincent, Midwesterner, anymore, either. There had to be a happy medium somewhere. She just hoped like hell she could find it.

She started to remember more, tiny details of things that might have been meaningless if she'd never lost her memory. She'd understood Felix's Spanish phrases that first night because Mrs. Montero had said things like that all the time. Her grandmother had taught her to make fig cookies. The reason she drank dirty martinis was because that was what her father drank—he'd instructed her on how to make them when she was in middle school so that she could be his home bartender. When she was old enough to go to bars herself, they'd become her go-to drink, even though she hadn't been that keen on them—not the way she liked Felix's mojitos. Marco had preferred Scotch and cognac, so she'd always had those on hand for him. She'd played basketball all through middle and high school, both JV and varsity. Her team had even gone to the state semifinals when she was a sophomore. And it had indeed been Carmen's quinceañera she had attended when they were both fifteen. She'd worn the pink frilly dress because Carmen had picked it out for her, and she loved her friend too much to disappoint her by not wearing it.

Rory covered her eyes with both hands, fighting back tears. "There's so much, Felix. There's just so much. I can't… I don't…" But her words and thoughts both trailed off before she could complete any of them.

"Hey, hey, hey," she heard him say. "It's okay, Rory."

He scooted closer to her, wrapped an arm around her shoulders and pulled her close. She melted into him, fighting back more tears. There really was just so much. So many memories. So many feelings. Too many memories. Too many feelings. Not the least of which was how this was going to change whatever was happening between her and Felix. Things had just started feeling pretty good between them. Now she was someone else. Someone with a past. Someone with a history. Someone he might not like as much as he'd liked her before. Because she was pretty sure he'd liked her before. Maybe even as much as she liked him.

He ran his hand slowly up and down her arm and settled his cheek on the crown of her head. Quietly, he said, "You know, it's no wonder your subconscious didn't want you to remember your life. At least the one you'd been living before your injury. And that's why the snippets you did get were only from times when you were happy."

She sniffled softly, nestling her head into the welcoming hollow between his chin and shoulder. Being with him like this felt like the first thing in her life to go right since… Well, since ever.

"I can't believe I was the woman I was when I had my accident," she said. "She was just so different from the woman I am now. I can't imagine how I ended up being that way. I just… I think I wanted to feel like I fit in somewhere, you know? After losing Carmen and her family, there was no place I felt like I belonged. Not until…"

She halted herself before she said too much and hastily concluded, "I just wanted to belong somewhere. And I guess I figured the only way to do that was to be someone I wasn't. So I became the person they all expected me to be. Wanted me to be. Even if it wasn't me at all."

"It doesn't matter who you were," Felix told her. "All that matters is who you are now. And that you know who you are now."

She did know that. In more ways than one. She knew she was Aurora Venturi of Elizabeth, New Jersey, by birth, and Rory Vincent of Endicott, Indiana, by choice. Even once she went back to using her legal last name, she'd still be Rory. Rory Venturi. A woman who loved flowers and cats and painting and mojitos and...

And Felix. Rory was a woman who loved Felix. And the way he made her feel. Right now, that was the only thing—the *only* thing—that mattered to her.

He was still sitting beside her, still had his arm wrapped around her waist, was still holding her close. When she turned to look at him, his face was a scant inch away from hers. For a moment, she only locked her gaze with his. Neither of them seemed to really know what to do next. So, acting purely on instinct, Rory tilted her head back and lifted her face to his, covering his mouth with hers.

He didn't hesitate to kiss her back. And in that moment, everything else fell away. All the confusion, all the fear, all the doubt. There was only Rory and Felix and everything that had passed between them. That was still passing between them. Enveloping them. Surrounding them.

For a while, all they did was sit close together and kiss as the cool night breeze washed over them, and the stars shone down from overhead. Little by little, though, Felix deepened the kiss, which Rory returned in kind. The arm around her waist wrapped tighter, pulling her closer still, and she felt the fingers of his other hand dip below her shirt, skimming the bare skin beneath. She curled one hand around his nape and cupped the other over his chest. Beneath her fingers, his heart was hammering hard—maybe even as hard as her own—and his chest rose and fell as his breathing deepened. Her own breaths were becoming wild and rough, and little splashes of heat ignited everywhere he touched her. But when he inched his hand higher, covering her breast, she cried out raggedly, pulling her mouth from his.

But Felix wasn't ready to stop and seized her lips again, tasting her even more deeply than before. He guided her so that she was on her back on the blanket then lay beside her. As she wound her arms around his waist to pull him closer, he levered his leg between both of hers, wedging it against the heated heart of her. Rory cried out again at the contact, moving a hand to the hard curve of his firm buttock to pull him closer still. She bucked against him once, twice, three times, and he dipped his mouth to her neck, dragging open-mouthed kisses along it and her shoulder.

Somehow, she found the presence of mind to whisper, "We should take this inside."

Somehow, Felix had the presence of mind to hear her. Because he lifted his head to look down at her. In the soft night light, she could see how his eyes had darkened, how his hair had gone wild from the twisting of her fingers, how his lips had become swollen with the fierceness of their kisses. He nodded.

"Yeah. I guess we should."

They scrambled up from the blanket, and Felix took Rory's hand in his. He started to lead them to the trap door that would take them to his place, but she stopped him.

"We're not doing this in your little twin bed," she told him, smiling. Then she silently tilted her head toward her place next door.

"Right," he said. "That would be a little more comfortable, wouldn't it?"

Oh, she wouldn't call what the two of them were about to enjoy *comfortable*. But she nodded anyway.

He took a step in that direction, then halted. "I do have to get something from my place first, though," he told her.

Before she could object, he was making his way quickly to the corner where his own roof access hatch was, disappearing into the square opening. A few minutes later, he reappeared, looking no different and acting as if nothing had happened at all. Then he took her hand in his and led her in the other direction. Neither said a word as they retreated. Felix helped her down the ladder and locked the roof access door afterward, then she led him to her apartment and locked that door behind them, too. She leaned back against it, needing a minute to regroup and prepare. But he clearly wasn't willing to wait. He slung one arm above her head and the other around her waist, then crowded his entire body against hers and kissed her again. And again. And again.

Somehow, Rory was able to skim off the jacket that was making her almost as hot as Felix was. Once it was gone, he followed suit, reaching behind himself to grab his shirt in one fist and yanking it over his head. He helped Rory out of hers next, so that they were both topless, then pushed himself against her again, back against the door, naked flesh to naked flesh. She gasped when she felt him swell hard against her belly, and he took advantage of her open mouth to thrust his tongue inside. Then he pushed his hand between them to palm her breast, rubbing his thumb across the rigid peak. She drove her hand behind him, pushing it beneath the waistband of his sweatpants, lowering it until she was cupping his hot skin, too.

Felix growled at the contact, dropping his hands to her pajama pants, pushing them down past her hips. Then he moved his hand between her legs and stroked her, dipping a slick finger inside her when she spread them wider. Had his body not still been pressed against hers, Rory would have crumpled on the spot. Instead, she went limp against him as wave after wave of sensation washed over her.

Vaguely, she registered Felix pulling her pants the rest of the way down and kneeling before her. But there was nothing vague about what he did next. Pushing her legs wider still, he moved his mouth to the damp folds of flesh between and tasted her. As she tangled her fingers in his hair to hold him there, he flicked his tongue against her, over and over, darting it gently against that that most sensitive tip. Clenching his hair tight, she cried out as another orgasm shook her. Then

Felix was standing again, scooping her up and carrying her to her bed.

And then she was on her belly, watching as he donned a condom that had been the thing he'd needed to retrieve from his place. He moved behind her, pulling her hips up higher so that she was on her knees, then entered her from behind. Again, Rory cried out at the contact. He was so… oh… And he filled her slowly…deeply…completely. All she could do was curl her fingers into the sheets and hang on as he drove himself into her, again and again and again. Then, somehow, she was on top of him, astride him, his hands covering her breasts as he thrust his hips upward. She bent down to kiss him, filling his mouth with her tongue this time, and he moved his hands to her hips. His thrusting grew wilder after that, until finally, finally, he let himself go over the edge, too, spending himself completely.

As one, they rolled to their sides, facing each other, gasping for breath and coherent thought. Then Felix smiled. And Rory smiled. And what few things about the night that hadn't yet fallen into place suddenly, silently, found their way there. She just wished she knew how long they would stay…

Chapter Thirteen

Long moments passed before either of them seemed willing or able to say anything. Rory struggled to think of something, anything, that might clarify where the two of them stood. Of course, it would help if she knew where they stood. Really, she supposed they'd been dancing around something like this happening since the day they met. That had been the day Felix and Tinima came to her shop to welcome her to the neighborhood with boxed lunches from La Mariposa for both her and Ezra, as they'd been putting the final touches on Wallflowers for their grand opening. He'd rapped on the jamb of the open back door, and Rory had spun around to see who was there. Her heart had plummeted to her belly the second she saw him, and the smile on his face had gone slack. In that instant, something had arced between the two of them, some weird recognition or awareness or knowledge or whatever, as if some cosmic thread had wrapped around them both and tethered them together forever.

At the time, she'd just chalked it up to the sort of instant physical attraction that could happen with people sometimes. Felix was a gorgeous and charismatic man. Naturally, Rory would feel an instant attraction to him.

Now, of course, she knew it was a lot more than that. Part of her felt like she had known Felix her entire life. Though, in a way, she supposed she had. She'd known him her entire life in Endicott. And of all the lives she'd lived—as a little girl who was the apple of her father's eye, as the teenager more at home with her best friend's family, as the adult woman trying to please everyone but herself—her life in Endicott was the happiest one she'd ever had. And a lot of that was because of Felix.

Since she didn't know what to say, she reached for his hand, weaving her fingers with his. He looked back at her, closing his hand over hers without hesitation, as if it was something they'd been doing for years. When she ran her thumb along the length of his, she felt a hard ridge beneath it and lifted it to see what it was. A scar. A fairly significant one. She'd never noticed it before. Then again, she'd never been this close to him.

She was grateful for having discovered the long-ago wound. It gave her something to say to him that would break the silence that had settled over them without them having to talk about anything important. Like what the future for the two of them held. If it held anything at all.

She bent her elbow so that their two hands rose between them, then stroked the scar again. "What happened here?" she asked.

She'd expected him to say something about a long-ago accident in the kitchen or a childhood injury from falling off a bike. Instead, the smile that had begun to curl his lips went flat, his entire body went stiff and the temperature around them seemed to plummet. What she had thought was an innocent question that might lead to an interesting anecdote that would lighten the veil of seriousness that was threatening to fall over them instead made it fall even faster.

"I'm sorry," she said, backpedaling. "If it's something you'd rather not talk about—"

"It is something I'd rather not talk about," he told her.

"Then you don't have to say any—"

"But I think it's something you should probably know."

She wasn't sure how to respond. He looked so somber, almost mournful. Without thinking, she brushed her thumb over the old injury again. When she did, Felix clumsily disentangled their fingers. Then he sat up in her bed to lean back against the headboard. So Rory did, too. She started to reach for him again, because she didn't want to break physical contact with him. But he lifted his hand in front of his face and stared at the scar.

"It happened when I was nine," he told her. "I had a friend back then. Named Megan."

She immediately remembered that Megan was the name of one of the sock puppets they'd found among his grandmother's things. The puppet who had been the maître d' of Felix's sock restaurant. The one whose name had been much less exotic than those of the other two. But she said none of this to him. Only waited for him to continue.

"Chance and Max aren't the only best friends I had when we were kids," he began again. "Megan was, too. Though maybe she was really more of a first crush than a best friend," he added. "But at that time in my life, I really didn't know what a crush was."

Rory hesitated a moment before asking, "What happened to her?"

"She died."

He spoke the two words so quickly, and so flatly, that something inside her clenched hard again.

He ran the index finger of his other hand along the scar. "Not long after this happened, actually."

"Felix, I'm so sorry," she said softly. She couldn't imagine the depth of grief and confusion a child must experience at losing a friend the same age. "Really, if you'd rather not talk about it, you don't have to."

Now he looked at her. He even managed a smile, though it wasn't exactly a cheerful one. Then he dropped his hands back to his side and, with the scarred one, wove his fingers through hers again. And that gesture, however small, eased a lot of the tension still coiled inside her.

"No, it really is something you should know," he said. "Because Megan died of an illness that made her lose her memory. I went to see her one day not long before she died, not realizing just how far along her illness was. And…" Here, he sighed heavily. "She had no idea who I was, Rory. She didn't remember me at all."

"Oh, Felix," she said. She squeezed his hand

tighter. "That must have been horrible for a little boy."

"It would have been horrible for anyone," he said. "But, yeah. It hit nine-year-old me pretty hard."

"I imagine it hits thirty-year-old you pretty hard, too," she said, knowing it was true. Maybe she'd just regained her memory, but she remembered, too well, how it had felt to be rejected by someone she loved when she was a child. Even now, it hurt. And she still had the chance to rebuild something with her father, if Nardo would let her. For Felix, with Megan, there would never be such an opportunity.

Rory listened as Felix told her about how Megan reacted that day when she didn't recognize him, about how she'd been so terrified, she'd hurled a lamp at him and cut his hand deeply enough to require stitches. Then he told her about not being able to see his friend again, since both his grandmother and Megan's parents hadn't thought it would be a good idea. And then he told her how Megan died not long after that, leaving him with a final memory of her that had been filled with fear and pain.

It all came together for Rory as he spoke. Why Felix had become so distant when she told him about her amnesia, and why he had been so reluctant to help her regain her memories when she asked. He'd feared she wouldn't regain them. The same way his childhood friend had never regained hers. Maybe, on some level, some part of him—probably the part that was nine years old—had even feared she might lose more of her memory. Might lose the part of it that included him. He'd been forgotten once by someone he cared about. He hadn't wanted to go through that again.

Which was maybe why he'd kept himself distant even after the two of them had become friends, too. Would he still keep himself distant, she wondered, now that she had her memory back and they were considerably more than friends?

"It's weird," he said when he finished his story, "but I still dream about her sometimes. Not very often, but…sometimes. There's a part of me that still misses her."

"I don't imagine that will ever go away," she said.

He turned to meet her gaze levelly. "No. I don't imagine it will."

Rory inhaled a shallow breath and held it. Then, very, very softly, she said, "You thought I might go away, didn't you?"

He didn't flinch at the question. But he didn't respond, either. Only studied her with something she couldn't quite decipher.

So she braved further, “You thought my amnesia might make me forget you.”

Still, he said nothing. But his gaze never left hers.

“That’s why you didn’t want to help me at first, isn’t it? Because I reminded you of Megan, and because you were afraid it would…” She hesitated. “You were afraid it would be the same way with me that it was with her.”

He still didn’t reply. Not with words, anyway. But she could see by the look in his eyes that on some level, she was right.

She squeezed his hand tight and told him, “Felix, I’m not going anywhere. I love it here in Endicott.” Of course, Endicott wasn’t the only thing she loved. She just wasn’t sure if she should tell him that.

His golden eyes darkened, but still, he said nothing.

She hesitated again. Then she thought, *What the hell?* What did she have to lose? In a way, she was starting a whole new life from this night on. She didn’t want to go back to being the woman she was before. She wanted to be the woman she’d become. One without artifice. One who was being true to herself and the people around her.

Even so, she still felt the need to skitter around what she really wanted to say. “Even when I was a kid, I don't think I ever really felt like I was where I was supposed to be. Where I wanted to be. That didn't happen until I came to Endicott. And until…until I met you, Felix."

For another long moment, his expression was impenetrable. Rory's heart, which had been pounding like a freight train, began to sink. He may have just made love to her, but maybe he didn't feel the same way she did. Maybe, to him, love had had nothing to do with it. But then why was she surprised? It wasn't like he'd voiced any heartfelt confessions to her or told her he couldn't live without her. He'd made clear from the start that he was only with her long enough to help her out. Sure, he may have warmed up to her over the past few days, but that didn't mean he was ready to make some major life change because of her. He'd made no secret about wanting to get out of Endicott. He'd told her over and over again how this wasn't the place where he belonged. How he'd been planning his escape since he was a teenager. How there was nothing here for him.

Finally, though, slowly, he began to smile. And little by little, something inside Rory began to smile, too.

"It is a nice town," he said. "And you do fit in here perfectly."

She couldn't help noticing that he said nothing about how he fit in here with her.

So, very cautiously, she said, "But it's not perfect for you, is it? You can't wait to get out of here. You can only be happy someplace big and exciting like Miami or New York. Someplace where interesting things happen all the time."

He expelled a sigh, one filled with satisfaction, relief and...happiness?

"Rory, Rory, Rory," he said. "How could anything be more interesting than an amnesiac woman from New Jersey who wears sequined halter tops and glitter platforms and has a father who may or may not be a mafia don, being plunked down in the middle of America's heartland, where she nurtures plants and bakes fig cookies? What could be more interesting than a woman who paints flowers and befriends derpy cats and plays basketball better than me? A woman who makes a man do nothing but think about her all damned day and dream about her all damned night?"

Her heart was near bursting with every word he spoke, but the only way she knew to respond was to smile and ask, "You think my father is a mafia don?"

"Fuhgeddaboudit," he told her with a chuckle. "We have more important things to talk about."

He smiled as he reached for her, pulling her close. "Later," he said, before dipping his head to kiss her again.

Felix and Rory slept late Friday morning. So late that they were awakened by a text from Tinima asking him where he was. Felix picked up his phone to text her back just as Rory jumped out of bed as if someone had taken a cattle prod to her. She grabbed last night's clothes from the floor and hastily began to dress.

"Oh, jeez, you're going to be late for work," she said as she shoved her arms through her shirtsleeves. "I am so sorry. I mean, Ezra can take care of things at Wallflowers since I usually go in late on Fridays anyway, but La Mariposa will be opening soon. You need to be there."

Felix watched her dress, sighing his resignation that there would clearly be no morning snuggles. Not that he normally indulged in morning snuggles. In fact, he always did his best to avoid morning snuggles with women because even the thought of morning snuggles had always made him want to gag. It was why he never, ever, spent the night at a woman's place, in her bed—just so he could prevent that very thing from happening. Well, he hadn't done that until last night, anyway, a realization that should have stunned him, but instead felt like the most natural thing in the world. Morning snuggles with Rory would have been fun. Among other things.

"What's your hurry?" he asked her as he texted back his chef de cuisine.

"You're going to be late," she repeated. "We need to get dressed."

He tossed his phone onto the nightstand. "Nah. I just told Tinima she's in charge of lunch and that I'll be down sometime this afternoon."

Rory stopped dressing, literally with one leg in her pajama pants and one leg out. "Are you sure you want to do that?" she asked.

"Do what?"

She gestured toward his phone. "What if Tinima needs you?"

"Please," he replied. "The woman could run the entire world if she wanted to. Which will actually be really helpful when I tell her she's going to be executive chef of the new La Mariposa. I just need to find a location. I'm thinking Miami. Her folks and sister live there. She'd love it."

He could tell Rory was clenching her teeth tight, probably to keep her mouth from dropping open in astonishment.

He grinned. "What?" he said. "I still want to open other La Mariposas in bigger markets. I just don't feel like I need to be the one in charge once they're up and running."

Rory eyed him dubiously. "You're joking, right?"

Hadn't he made clear last night that he wasn't leaving Endicott any more than she was? He thought he had. He replayed their conversation as well as he could and realized maybe he hadn't said in so many words that he was staying here.

So he met her gaze levelly and, in the most serious voice he could muster, told her, "I am not joking."

She still didn't look convinced. "You're abandoning your plans to leave Endicott?" she asked. "Just like that?"

"Rory, why would I leave Endicott, when everything I want—everything I need—is right here?"

Her entire body seemed to go limp at that. Even so, she asked, "What about your Michelin star?"

Now he smiled. "Oh, that."

"Yeah, that."

"Well, you know, I'm not ruling it out. I couldn't be in all of my restaurants all of the time, anyway. They don't award those stars based specifically on the chef. They award them based on the food and whether or not the spirit of the chef is present in them. As long as my other Mariposas are cooking my recipes and putting the proper spin on them, that's all that matters." He thought for a moment—while Rory stared at him in amazement. "Actually, Tinima putting her little touches on some dishes could also be a very good thing. Besides," he added, "there are other kinds of stars that are more important than Michelin's."

Like the stars they'd been looking at last night, when everything suddenly fell into place to allow Rory to regain her memory. Everything had fallen into place for Felix last night, too. The stars they'd been looking at last night were lucky stars. Stars he figured it was probably best not to mess with.

Before she could reply to that, however, there was a loud pounding at the exterior front door. So loud, in fact, that they glanced at each other in alarm. So loud that Felix, too, rose from bed and tugged on his clothes from the night before.

When the pounding sounded a second time, Rory looked at him with concern. "That doesn't sound good."

"No, it doesn't," he agreed.

Together, they went to the door. It would be pretty clear to whomever was on the other side that they'd spent the night together—and oh, what a night it had been—so both were a little cautious as they stepped through Rory's front door and approached the exterior door. Felix was about to check the peephole when the pounding erupted a third time, even more furiously than before, so he instinctively just jerked the door open, wearing the most threatening expression he could summon.

When he saw Frankie standing on the other side of the door, however, wearing his usual tracksuit and with his hair slicked back with enough oil to toss a Caesar salad, Felix's animosity ebbed. Mostly because Frankie was holding a cat carrier with a smoky gray cat inside that looked more than a little worried about the situation.

"Sage!" Rory cried from behind him.

She pushed past Felix to retrieve the carrier from Frankie's hand, then bolted back into her apartment. Felix heard the cat meow furiously in response, but instead of opening the door to the carrier, she only cooed soft words to him to calm him down. Probably didn't want to risk him bolting through the open door and escaping into the wilds of Endicott, where she might never find him again.

"Thank God it's really you," Frankie said to her retreating figure. "That cat is the most malevolent animal I've ever had the misfortune to travel with." He mimicked a theatrical *ptui*. "Good riddance."

Or maybe Rory didn't release Sage because

she knew he'd dismember Frankie piece by piece, since the guy didn't exactly seem like a cat person.

"What do you want?" Felix asked him.

"Just to bring Aurora her cat," he replied. "And to deliver a message from her father."

The last part of his comment immediately brought Rory back to the door. "What message?" she asked. Then she looked at him again, harder. "Hey, I remember you now," she said.

Frankie's chest puffed up at that. "Yeh, you should," he stated with all the confidence of an anonymous teenage boy on the internet.

"But wait, not as Frankie," Rory added. "You have a nickname. 'Finger Guns,' right? You're Finger Guns Conte."

Felix turned to look at her, incredulous. "His mob nickname is 'Finger Guns?'"

Rory looked back at him, just as disbelieving. "Why do you keep thinking my father is a mobster? I told you. He's a businessman."

Instead of answering her, Felix turned back to Frankie. "Frankie 'Finger Guns' Conte? That was the best you could do?"

Now Frankie looked a little put off. "Okay, so it's not the best nickname. All the good ones were already taken, you know? You got your Vinnie the Knife, your Mikey the Shiv, your Joey Blue

Eyes… Big Tony, Little Tony, Tony Cannoli… 'Finger Guns' was pretty much all that was left. And it's a perfectly good name, too," he hurried to add. "Especially for someone who's Nardo Venturi's second-in-command."

Rory shook her head. "You're not my father's second-in-command. Guido 'the Grim Reaper' Russo is the vice president of Venturi Holdings."

"Grim Reaper?" Felix echoed. "Oh, now, that's a good nickname."

Rory nodded. "Yeah. Finger Guns here actually works at a meatpacking plant in Union Square."

Felix couldn't help noticing that the more she talked to Frankie, the stronger her New Jersey accent was becoming. If she kept this up, she was going to need a mob nickname, too.

"The packing plant is just my night job," Frankie assured them. "During the day I'm—"

"During the day, you deliver pints from my father's ice cream parlor," Rory said.

"Hey, do you know what's really in those pints I'm deliverin'?" Frankie demanded.

Felix figured it would be best if neither he nor Rory found out the answer to that question. So he interjected, "Look, Frankie, what are you doing here besides delivering Sage?"

He shrugged, but there was nothing careless in

the gesture. "Nardo's been lookin' for Aurora for a while now. Marco told 'im she canceled their wedding over Christmas and left Chicago, that she took off with some mook named Einar to go to Reykjavik, and he ain't seen her since. And because Nardo is smart enough to know there ain't no such place as Reykjavik, he arranged for Marco to wake up with a cabbage head in his bed."

"Cabbage head?" Felix echoed, confused. "Don't you mean horse head?"

Frankie recoiled. "No, I mean cabbage head."

"Marco's vegan," Rory added, as if that explained everything. Actually, all it did was confuse Felix even more.

"Anyway," Frankied continued, looking at Rory now, "your father then sent out a search party to look for you. They finally tracked you down through the jewelry you pawned to buy your shop, and Nardo sent me to make sure it was you. He said if I find you, he'll maybe move me up in the family business."

"I thought you were already his right-hand man," Felix pointed out.

"And you're not in my family," Rory added.

"Hey, I said '*maybe*,'" Frankie reminded them. He continued, "But even after I found you, I still couldn't believe it was you. I mean, you don't look nothin' like Aurora Venturi no more. I cannot believe you cut your hair off. You had great hair."

"That was why you broke into my apartment," Rory said, sounding surprisingly unbothered by the realization. "To find some kind of evidence that it was me."

Frankie nodded. "And there it was, right under your bed. I remember you wore that halter top at Thanksgiving at your dad's place. You were smokin' hot that night." He pursed his lips, closed his eyes and did one of those chef's kisses that always made Felix's eye twitch.

He cleared his throat with as much menace as he could.

"Right," Frankie said. "Anyway, when I sent photos of all the stuff I found to your father, he was very relieved you were okay."

Rory seemed surprised by Frankie's assurance. "My father wants me to come home?" she asked. Almost hopefully, Felix couldn't help noticing.

"Oh, God, no," Frankie told her. "He just wanted to make sure you were still alive, because he didn't wanna have to, you know, avenge your death. I mean, what would the neighbors think if he just let the guy off the hook who mur—"

"Who hurt his daughter in some way," Felix hastened to finish for him. Since he honestly didn't want to know any more than he already suspected about Rory's life back East.

Frankie looked at him as if he were an idiot, but shrugged again. "Yeh. But no. He don't want you to come back to Elizabeth. He was gettin' tired of you showin' up on Page Six all the time, bringin' *waaaay* too much attention to the family. Once I told Nardo I found you, and you were workin' as a florist in Indiana—once he stopped laughin', I mean—he told me to tell you he'll pay off your mortgage on the shop and send you a check every month if you promise not to come home."

He looked both Rory and Felix up and down. "Though maybe it's all moot, 'cause lookin' at youse right now, it don't look like you wanna come back to Jersey, anyway."

"I don't," Rory confirmed.

"So we're good then," Frankie said.

"We will be," Rory replied. "Once you tell my father I don't want his money. But I do want to come see him. He and I need to talk. About a lot of things."

Frankie lifted both hands in front of him in mock surrender. "Whatever. That's between you and him. Me, I'm just happy to be gettin' outta this one-diner town." He looked at Rory again, shaking his head. "How can you like it here? This place is so…so clean and decent. So wholesome. It makes my skin crawl."

And without waiting for further comment—not that he seemed to need further comment—Frankie spun on his heels and trotted down the stairs. Felix and Rory watched as he jogged down the alley and around the corner, disappearing into the unsullied sanctuary of Endicott, Indiana. Wordlessly, they then closed the door and returned to the apartment. Sage was looking at them curiously from inside her carrier, but only offered a soft, inquisitive, *"Mrph?"*

"That was the weirdest exchange I've ever had," Felix said to the room at large. "And hell, I've had exchanges with a woman who has amnesia."

Rory smiled at that. "Not anymore, she doesn't."

Felix smiled back. "Why do you think that is?" he asked. "What made you suddenly remember everything last night the way you did?"

Immediately, she replied, "Your kiss."

Her answer surprised him. "What, I'm Prince Charming?"

She laughed lightly. "Hardly."

Yeah, okay. He hadn't exactly been a prince among men when Rory first asked for his help. He had his whole life to make up for that. Because he wasn't going anywhere. Not without her.

She covered the two steps necessary to bring her close to him, then looped her arms around his neck. He, in turn, wrapped his arms around her waist.

"When you kissed me last night," she said softly, "it just made me feel so…good. So happy. Happy in a way I've never been happy before. Without worry about anything. Without fear that I wasn't measuring up. In that moment, everything just felt right. No matter what had happened before. No matter what might happen next. You made me happy in that moment, Felix. That was all that mattered. And I think once I was happy, my brain just said, 'Okay then.' And it gave me back everything I'd been missing. Because, suddenly, with or without my memories, there was nothing missing at all. Because there was you."

Felix nodded. He actually understood that. Because he'd kind of felt the same way when he kissed her. Everything just fell into place perfectly in that moment. He finally knew his life's purpose. Building a life with Rory. Even better, he knew where he belonged. Right here, at home, in Endicott. Home that finally felt like home, all because of a comet that granted a wish. All because of a woman who made things more than a little interesting.

"I love you, Felix Suarez," that woman told him now.

"I love you, Aurora Venturi," he replied.

"Rory," she corrected him with a grin. "Call me Rory."

He grinned back. "Nice to meet you, Rory."

And, *dios mío*, he couldn't wait to get to know her better.

* * * * *

Keep an eye out for the next
Lucky Stars romance from Elizabeth Bevarly,

Secret under the Stars

Coming in November 2022!

#2941 THE CHRISTMAS COTTAGE

Wild Rose Sisters • by Christine Rimmer

Alexandra Herrera has her whole life mapped out. But when her birth father leaves her an unexpected inheritance, she impulsively walks away from it all. And now that she's snowed in with West Wright, she learns that lightning really *can* strike twice. So much, in fact, that the sparks between them could melt any ice storm…if only they'd let them!

#2942 THANKFUL FOR THE MAVERICK

Montana Mavericks: Brothers & Broncos • by Rochelle Alers

As a rodeo champion, Brynn Hawkins is always on the road, but something about older, gruff-but-sexy rancher Garrett Abernathy makes her think about putting down roots. As Thanksgiving approaches, Brynn fears she's running out of time, but she's determined to find her way into this calloused cowboy's heart!

#2943 SANTA'S TWIN SURPRISE

Dawson Family Ranch • by Melissa Senate

Cowboy Asher Dawson and rookie cop Katie Crosby had the worst one-night stand ever. Now she's back in town with his two babies. He won't risk losing Katie again—even as he tries to deny their explosive chemistry. But his marriage of convenience isn't going as planned. Maybe it's time to see what happens when he moves his captivating soul mate beyond friendship…

#2944 COUNTDOWN TO CHRISTMAS

Match Made in Haven • by Brenda Harlen

Rancher Adam Morgan's hands are full caring for his ranch and three adorable sons. When his custody is challenged, remarriage becomes this divorced dad's best solution—and Olivia Gilmore doesn't mind a proposal from the man she's loved forever. But Adam is clear: this is a match made by convenience. But as jingle bells give way to wedding bells, will he trust in love again?

#2945 SECRET UNDER THE STARS

Lucky Stars • by Elizabeth Bevarly

When his only love, Marcy Hanlon, returns, Max Tavers believes his wish is coming true. But Marcy has different intentions—she secretly plans to expose Max as the cause of her wealthy family's downfall! She'll happily play along and return his affections. But if he's the reason her life went so wrong, why does being with him feel so right?

#2946 A SNOWBOUND CHRISTMAS COWBOY

Texas Cowboys & K-9s • by Sasha Summers

Rodeo star Sterling Ford broke Cassie Lafferty's heart when he chose a lifestyle of whiskey and women over her. Now the reformed party boy is back, determined to reconnect with the woman who got away. When he rescues Cassie and her dogs from a snowstorm, she learns she isn't immune to Sterling's smoldering presence. But it'll take a canine Christmas miracle to make their holiday romance permanent!

By the book success story Alexandra Herrera's got it all mapped out. But when her birth father leaves her an unexpected inheritance, she impulsively walks away from her entire life! And now that she's snowed in with West Wright, she learns that lightning really can strike twice. So much, in fact, that the sparks between them could melt any ice storm...if only they'd let them!

Read on for a sneak peek at
The Christmas Cottage,
the latest in the Wild Rose Sisters series
by New York Times *bestselling author Christine Rimmer!*

So that was an option, just to say that she needed her alone time and West would intrude on that. Everyone would understand. But then he would stay at the Heartwood Inn and that really wasn't right…

And what about just telling everyone that it would be awkward because she and West had shared a one-night stand? There was nothing unacceptable about what she and West had done. No one here would judge her. Alex and West were both adults, both single. It was nobody's business that they'd had sex on a cold winter night when he'd needed a friend and she was the only one around to hold out a hand. It was one of those things that just happen sometimes.

It would be weird, though, to share that information with the family. Weird and awkward. And Alex still hoped she would never have to go there.

HSEEXP0922

"Alex?" Weston spoke again, his voice so smooth and deep and way too sexy.

"Hmm?"

"You ever plan on answering my question?"

"Absolutely." It came out sounding aggressive, almost angry. She made herself speak more cordially. "Yes. Honestly. There's plenty of room here. You're staying in the cottage. It's settled."

"You're so bossy..." He said that kind of slowly—slowly and also naughtily—and she sincerely hoped her cheeks weren't cherry red.

"Weston." She said his name sternly as a rebuke.

"Alexandra," he mocked.

"That's a yes, right?" Now she made her voice pleasant, even a little too sweet. "You'll take the second bedroom."

"Yes, I will. And it's good to talk to you, Alex. At last." Did he really have to be so...ironic? It wasn't like she hadn't thought more than once of reaching out to him, checking in with him to see how he was holding up. But back in January, when they'd said goodbye, he'd seemed totally on board with cutting it clean. "Alex? You still there?"

"Uh, yes. Great."

"See you day after tomorrow. I'll be flying down with Easton."

"Perfect. See you then." She heard the click as he disconnected the call.